King's Bride

A Reverse Harem Dragon Fantasy

Ava Sinclair

Pandora's Box
Publishing

Contents

Chapter One

ZARA

You will be a lovely queen.

"No"

Yes. You will be the bride of a great and powerful king.

"No. I don't want to be. You can't make me."

The pale face staring from under the hood is menacing, its dark eyes devoid of pity or understanding.

"Let me die. Just let me die." My voice is weary as I turn my head away. "I will never marry your dragon."

The hooded man smiles. *I told you. He will not be a dragon when he marries you. He will be a man.*

In the distance I hear a rumble and the clatter of rocks. The dragon is coming.

"He is a beast." Tears of fear and anger sting my eyes. "He will always be a beast. I will never marry him. You cannot make me."

The eyes under the hood narrow. *That was foolish, my dear. Now you've made him angry.* The hooded figure steps back, and through the iron bars of my cage I see something glowing red in the dark precipice below.

"No." I begin to whimper. "I'm sorry!"

But it is too late. The cavern reverberates with the sound of the dragon's growl and in the distance I hear the terrified screams of the other maidens. Even though we've been separated, they still cry out in fear when they hear the ShadowFell.

He is coming. His head is huge and covered in spikes; two large horns curl back towards the outstretched neck. His long body undulates as he moves, the great hooks on his wing joints grappling to snag the rocks as he edges towards me.

"Don't! Please don't!"

I know what's coming. I can smell the dragon's sulfurous breath. I can hear the hooded man chanting the incantation that will allow me to be consumed by dragon fire without dying. I fall to the floor of the cage, moving to the far edge. I grab the bars and scream. I can hear the mother maidens sobbing and calling my name.

The dragon has reached the ledge. It's waiting for me to turn and look. I know what I'll see if I do — the great maw of its mouth, the fire blazing at the back of its throat. I beg the gods to release me from this torment.

The dragon growls, the sound ancient and gravely. I turn, holding onto the cage as it inhales, the intake of air so powerful it threatens to pull me away from bars I grip for dear life.

"Noooo!" I scream, knowing there is no inhale without a fiery exhale.

Heat engulfs me as the dragon roars, exhaling flame. The force of his anger reverberates through the cavern; I am vaguely aware of the rocks falling all around the cage. But I can only feel now. I writhe and scream. Words cannot describe what it is like to be burned alive and not be saved by death.

"Zara! Zara!"

Hands. Cool hands. I am sitting on a bed, staring into the face of my sister. Sweat has plastered my gown to my body. My breath comes in ragged gasps. I begin to cry and Isla wraps her arms around me, covering my tear-stained face with kisses.

"It's okay. You're here. You're safe."

I'm shaking. I can still smell the sulfur and when I hold up my hands, I almost expect to see melted flesh fall away from bone instead of smooth white skin.

"Bad dreams again?" Isla searches my face. She's not left my side since I came here. "Do you remember them this time?"

"No." It's a lie. The dreams are getting more frequent and detailed, so much so that I've come to see them for what they are—repressed memories of my time with the ShadowFell. I rise from the bed and head to the wash basin across the room. I dip my hands in the cool water, splashing it on my face.

Water. The feel of it triggers a memory: a stream running down the rock I'm chained to. I put my tongue to the stream, lapping it eagerly. I'm in the dark, and around me I can hear the whispers and soft sobbing of other women, but I cannot see them.

"It's a big day for you, Zara." Isla's words bring me back to the present. I put a towel to my face.

"Yes, I know." I turn back to her.

She smiles. "I've picked your dress. I hope you don't mind."

"Of course not." I pile my hair up on my head, affixing it with two pins. It's damp with sweat. "You always had a better eye for clothes than I did, especially now that you are a lady."

"I may be a lady, but you're going to be a queen!" Isla puts a hand to my face. "My own little sister, Queen Zara of the Drakoryan Empire." She hugs me. "Think on it. Four strong men to protect you. Four princes who will take to the skies to battle not just for the crown, but for *you*!"

She steps back, searching my face. I know what she's looking for. Expectation. Excitement. Anything but the haunted look I try to hide.

"They will never let anyone hurt you again, Zara."

I manage the smile I know she wants to see. I have to be strong, or at least pretend to be. I have to be perfect, or at least the image of perfection. The Drakoryans saved me. I owe them my life, and that's what I'm about to give them.

Chapter Two

PRINCE BYMIR

M ount Fra'hir. Mount Za'Vol. Mount Jo'lyn. Mount Im'Ryl. Mount Gro'han.

I stare out at them from where I stand at the uppermost ridge of the tallest mountain of all, the Mountain of Kings.

Each mountain ringing the valley of the Drakoryan Empire — and there are many—lends its name to the lords who make it their own. The mountain castle is where they take their bride and raise sons.

The Mountain of Kings is different. The first king to rule here was King Arok, who bested his brothers Dax and Yrn for the crown and the right to claim Genev, the first Drakoryan queen. Arok's brothers remained as princes, successors to is crown should he die before their sons could battle for the right to rule.

No king has died before old age. Even before the last ShadowFell battle that claimed his life, our father King Vukuris, often told us he dreamt of the Long Sleep. Our kind, being neither man nor beast, do not go to the Sunlit Isle, but if that troubled Vukurcis, he did not show it. He had a good and long life, he said, and was tired. He was ready for rest.

I cannot get the image out of my mind—our mighty father, his life's blood spraying from his throat—plummeting to his death. I cannot forget the feeling of joining my brothers to breathe the fire that consumed both his body and the funeral pyre.

No mortal man can summit the Mountain of Kings. Only a dragon can reach the top. This morning I flew up through the frozen mist to land on a ledge and then shifted back into my human form. I am here for two reasons— to think, and because the direction of the wind sweeping up the peak blows dust and ash into the sky, where it floats past. I put my hand out, looking at the particles that land on my palm. Is this bit of gray dust part of my father? I close my hand and draw it to my chest. Drakoryans do not weep like women, especially Drakoryan princes. But it is hard not to feel bleak. The humans in the valley look at us in awe and with no small measure of envy. But right now, what I would not give to be fully human, if only to imagine my father in the Sunlit Isle, looking down on me and my brothers.

"If only you could tell us what to do, Father King," I say into the ashy wind that swirls past, pushing apart clouds to reveal the neighboring Mystic Mountain, the split in its side gaping like a wound. The sight of it brings fresh pain. We failed to protect it; the enemy plundered its magic, driving the witches that called it home Inward.

What would my father, the King, say if he were here? He'd tell me the past is something that happened, but the future is something we shape. He'd tell me that war is inevitable so long as evil is in the world. He'd remind me our curse comes with responsibilities. The ones who created the Drakoryans did not give us the option of ending our bloodline by choice. We are compelled to continue our destiny. Defiance of that destiny is not an option.

These were just words when I was a little thing at the king's knee. Now that he is dead, I know the truth in them. The desire to take a mate is strongest in Drakoryan royalty, where more is at stake than just the claiming of a virgin.

I wonder, did my father sacrifice himself when he went into battle? He consulted with the oracle Ezador many a night, and towards the end expressed an increased interest in divination. Did he know the ShadowFell's attack on the witches' sacred space would drain the enemy? Did my father, weaker with age, foresee this? Did he time his death so that a new king could be installed before the enemy returned?

My brothers and I all think it so. We discussed it in the wake of his death. But as the fire of his funeral pyre had cooled, another had started in his sons. We can barely stand the sight of one another now, but tonight we will have to endure one another's company as, for the first time, we greet the woman we will claim as our queen.

It will be our final peaceful moment before we take to the skies to battle for her and the right to rule this empire.

Chapter Three

ZARA

My sister has decided I should wear a heather green gown, with a split front revealing an underskirt of ivory shot through with golden threads. The bell sleeves are lined with the same ivory fabric, the ends so long that they hang to my knees.

Isla frets as her maid pulls the strings on my bodice.

"You're still so thin, Zara."

I look away, feeling guilty. Winter's icy grip has eased somewhat. Hunting and foraging has enabled the villagers and Drakoryans alike to stretch stores of food, and there is now hope that it may last until first planting and harvest. Food is still rationed, though, except for mine. I am to be queen, and must regain my strength. To hear my sister fret over my slight form makes me feel like a failure.

She is instantly solicitous. "I'm sorry. It is not your fault. You are fuller than you were." She pauses. "Zara. I always said I would kill the ShadowFell that burned our village and took you and the others. That hasn't changed."

"You're so fierce, Isla. I think you should be queen."

"Don't say that." She takes my hands. "Besides, my lords would be entirely lost if I were to leave them, and not at all understanding."

"They do love you. I can see it in their eyes." I pause. "Isla, Lord Turin told me the moment he saw you that he knew you were meant for him and his brothers. Do you think it will be the same for me, when I meet Bymir and his brothers?"

"*Princes*, Zara." Her correction is firm but gentle. "You must address them as such. Prince Bymir, Prince Rargi, Prince Yrgi, and Prince Oneg. Once you are claimed, you may call them by their names. Until then, you must defer to them as royalty." My sister steps back. "You look so beautiful."

"You didn't answer my question. Do you think they will love me, or is it as the servants whisper?"

Zara narrows her eyes. "What do they whisper?"

"That the princes are only taking me to deny the ShadowFell king my hand."

She turns away. "You listen to too much talk, Zara. This isn't the village."

"There's truth in gossip, sister. You said so many times yourself." I take hold of her. "Isla, you've always been my protective older sister, but don't protect me from the truth. I don't want to greet these princes feeling like some starry-eyed little fool when they only see me as some prize snatched from the enemy."

"Zara..." My sister sighs. "Come here."

She takes my hand and guides me to a window seat. It overlooks a ravine, and the view makes me dizzy. The abyss reminds me of my life. From the day I woke up here, I've felt like my existence was a void waiting to swallow me up. I have no more control than if I were falling into the chasm below. Her words do nothing to help matters.

"It's true. I will not lie to you. The ShadowFell killed King Vukuris. Now they must pay a price. They, too, must lose something precious. Seadus, the enemy king, intended you to be his bride. There is something special in you, more special than all the other maidens. The princes will have you for their own."

"So they'll mate with me to soothe their spite?" I stand from the seat and turn back to her, crossing my arms.

Isla fixes me with the same disapproving look I would get from her at home whenever she was about to give me some advice for my own good.

"Listen to me, little sister. Whether it be spite or lust, privilege or want of peace, Drakoryans have taken village women since the dawn of time. We women cannot control this fact. But we can control how we cope. I did not go gently to the beds of my lords. I made them earn my favors. No Drakoryan can force a woman to his bed, not even a prince. So while you may be—as you fear—a bride taken for spite, that does not mean they will not have to win you." She puts her hand on my belly. "Their future lies here. Within your little womb. No matter how royal or arrogant, they know this."

Tell me. Tell me when I become man that you will come to my bed. A voice, deep and gravelly, invades my thoughts. A memory. I feel a flush of heat on my face. My sister is calling my name, but it sounds strangely distant.

"Zara!" Her wavering image comes back into view. "Are you all right?"

It takes all my strength not to shudder. *Stop*, I silently beg my mind. *Please stop.* "I'm fine. Just suddenly hungry." I look past her to where a bowl of dried fruit sits on a table. "Do you think I could nibble a bit of something. And maybe have some water?"

"Of course." She kisses my cheek and hastens off to fetch me the last bite of food I'll enjoy before heading to the Mountain of Kings.

Chapter Four

PRINCE RARGI

I have been thinking of what it will be like, having a female. Not claiming one—I know well enough what that is like. Drakoryan males sow their seed far and near among the serving class, never having to worry about producing bastards. Our seed only takes root in our mate, and only after all brothers in a family have claimed her, and then only after the Deepening that binds us in thought.

I know the feel of a woman. I know how to trace the curves of her body to make her sigh, where to dip and delve and probe to make her moan. I know how to use my tongue and cock to make her beg, then beg for more. What I don't know is how to *be* with a woman, what to say. I was small when my mother died of a fever that even the healing pools could not cure. The witches were apologetic when they told my father that it was Fate taking her, that when a human has run her course of days, not even the pools can bring her back.

The day they took my mother's body away was the only day I saw my father cry, if that is even the word for that kind of grief. He tore through the castle, screaming one word —No!— over and over. He tore at his clothes and burst into flame in the great hall, the transformation so fierce as to crack the rocks as he tore his way outside. It took magic to fix the rift, and the witches made him promise never to do such a thing again.

I run my hand over the crack, trying to imagine the kind of love that can do that, that can send a dragon through the side of a mountain. My brothers and I have looked upon all the ladies of the Drakoryan Empire, fair jewels all. I will not deny that a few of them stirred my lust, and I felt jealous to think of the long winter nights they spent pleasuring their mates. But I never thought of the other things women offer, like companionship and conversation.

My father taught me to be a dragon. My mother taught me to be human. At court, she would encourage me to talk to strangers. It was easy enough, she said, and good practice for future rulers. Just find something in common, she told me.

I stare at the crack on the wall. The ShadowFell killed my king and Zara's parents. It hardly seems the basis for a relationship, but at least we hate the same dragons.

"Rargi!"

I turn at the sound of my name to see Ezador the Wise enter the room. He's been holed up in his tower more often than not since our father died. Even though there's no one else in the hall now but me, he still manages to make an entrance.

"Look at you," I say. "The witches have gone Inward and you squander magic to make yourself beautiful."

"So, you find me beautiful do you?" A brow arches on the perfect face beneath the hood. He sighs. "I'm afraid it's no use, Prince Rargi. My heart belongs to a strapping young soldier, for the moment at least. And even if I did fancy you, you're about to take a mate."

Only Ezador, Oracle to the Kings, could get away with such impertinence.

"Careful," I say. "Lest I track your soldier down and tell him that beneath the glamor is a wizened old man."

"Bah..." He waves me off. "Let me have my fun, Prince Rargi. There is so little to be had in these times that the only solace I find is in my looking glass." His tone grows serious. "I feel her approaching, your virgin. Do you sense her?"

I don't know. I look back at the crack on the wall. "I've been thinking on how she was left to wander in the woods under a spell, nearly starved. They say she doesn't remember her time with the ShadowFell."

Ezador's reply is quiet. "Yes. They do. They do say that."

"They also say she's weak and thin. It'll be like bedding a pile of twigs. How will she be able to handle a dragon's lust?"

"They are not so frail as they seem, these humans. And remember, this one survived her time with King Seadus."

"Don't call him that." I wheel around, not even trying to hide my anger.

But the oracle is unfazed. "Why not? Like it or not, Prince Rargi, Seadus is indeed king of the enemy horde. He has found the deep magic. You will have to deal with him both as a dragon and a man." He turns away. "In more ways than one."

"Speaking in riddles again, are we?" I'm irritated at myself for taking the bait. It's what he wanted, after all.

"Life is a riddle, my arrogant prince. Sometimes the answer comes in the most unassuming forms, and lessons from dark places we never knew existed." He waves a hand, using the magic that keeps him beautiful to open the door. "You should get to the throne room. The others are already seated and ready to meet the bride of the future king."

Chapter Five

ZARA

The entire village of Branlock could fit inside this room. I would be overwhelmed if I did not already know what these men are. They are dragons. Dragons need space, room to prowl, room to curl their long bodies around corners, room to thrash their serpentine tails and raise their long necks upwards so they can look down on the likes of my kind.

This is the largest castle, Isla tells me, because in the old days the Drakoryans were seeking to control their shifts. Uncontrolled emotion could cause them to turn from man to dragon without warning, and the rooms and tunnels of the Mountain of Kings were made especially large to accommodate two arguing brothers who might shift into beasts in any hall or hallway. There is something in the royal bloodline, she says, that still makes their shifts harder to control.

"Even if it was made for dragons, it seems like too much room." I can't stop thinking of how massive the mountain was as we approached.

"That too, is for a reason," my sister explains. "In the early days, it was not uncommon for princes to each take a bride, or even more than one if they chose. Not all the princes could be king, so from time to time there were battles determining who would hold the Mountain of Kings. Those who lost became lords. They got their own mountain, but only one family could rule."

"But today brothers take but one bride," I say. "Why?"

"Because long ago the witches determined the number of hungry dragons could reach unsustainable levels, so the order was reversed. Sharing a mate meant each dragon could father a son, but the population would grow more slowly."

"Getting a lesson in Drakoryan history?" Lady Lyla of Fra'hir joins us, looking resplendent in a red velvet gown. The front is stretched tight over her swollen belly. She is heavy with child, and her belly is larger than I'd think for just being halfway along and find myself wondering if Drakoryan babies grow larger. I glance at my own stomach, flat as a board. I can't imagine it swelling so.

"You'll need a knowledge of this culture, now that you're to be queen," Lady Lyla says, and I raise my eyes from her swollen middle. Like my sister, she looks content, despite the fact that we are at war.

"I will try, my lady," I say.

I find myself introduced to more and more lords and ladies. They clasp my hands and compliment me on my bravery. It seems everyone in the empire has been apprised of what I suffered in the grip of the ShadowFell, how I was put under a spell and left to be discovered by the Drakoryan, how when it was determined that only witch magic could save me I was taken to the Mystic Mountain by those unaware that I secretly housed the powerful magic that opened it from within.

I had expressed fear to my sister before coming here. Were it not for me, the ShadowFell would not have been able to enter the Mystic Mountain and access the deep magic of the pools to become half-man as the Drakoryan are.

I smile politely as I am introduced to family after family, each with seemingly more knowledge of my ordeal than I have.

A horn sounds, and everyone stops talking. "Lords and Ladies of the Drakoryan Empire!" I can hear the voice of the castle crier, but cannot see him. "Make way for the sons of the fallen King Vukurcis, long may he reign in the heart of man and dragon. Make way for the Princes Bymir, Rargi, Yrgi, and Oneg.

The lords and ladies bow their heads but do not bend the knee; that gesture is reserved for the king. Even though I am to be their mate, at the moment I am just another subject with her head lowered in obeisance, although I do raise my eyes as they pass.

They are large and wear the traditional leather skirts, but with ornate tunics bound about the middle by belts etched with dragon insignia. Their legs are muscular and booted. Each wears a prince's crown, but on the seat of a conspicuously empty throne is the king's crown they will fight for. I have to remind myself that they will also fight for me. It still seems as unreal as a dream.

The princes' thrones are on either side of the empty one that belonged to the fallen king. Two brothers go left, two go right, and only when they are seated does the crier tell us to lift our eyes and look upon the Sons of Vukurcis, which I have already done.

A man walks up the steps now, or glides. His motions are so fluid as to make it hard to determine how he's moving, and when he turns I cannot help but stare at the most beautiful face I have ever seen.

"Ezador, the king's oracle," my sister whispers in my ear. "He uses magic to make himself comely. But don't let his youthful beauty fool you. He is cunning and wise and as respected as the kings he's served."

I crane my neck to see. The oracle's silvery eyes scan the room. I feel a sudden shiver as they lock on me. A smile plays on his full lips and my heart twists. It's a comforting smile and I feel suddenly calm and at ease. I know he's working magic on me from where he stands, but I do not care. I am strangely grateful for it.

"Lords and Ladies of the Drakoryan Empire..." His words rise and fall like a melody as he stretches out his hands. "As decreed by law, when the ashes of the old king have blown to the four corners of the valley, from his seed a new king will rise. But not just a new king, but a new queen—a virgin captured, a virgin saved, a virgin exalted to the throne as bride to all and queen to one."

"Bride to all, queen to one." The crowd repeats his words and the oracle stretches out his hands again. As he does, I gasp. I can feel the warmth of a hand on mine. It's his hand, and yet he is at the front of the room. I see mine raised as I'm lifted from my seat. I look helplessly at Isla, who nods for me to approach the dais.

My heart thuds against my too-sharp breastbone. I feel small as I look up the aisle, towards the powerful princes who sit on each side of the empty throne.

While the princes all recognized the old king as father, they were actually sired by four different brothers. King Vukuris outlived his brothers, just as he outlived the queen. In the men before me, I see the same small build. But I also see the differences in parentage.

Isla told me they are seated in order of birth, so the one farthest to the left would be Prince Bymir. He has a close-cropped beard, brown like his hair that curls to the top of his shoulders. His nose is slightly hawkish, giving him a predatory look. His mouth is wide, and I think he would have a big smile. But he is not smiling. His arms and chest are broad under his tunic. One hand grips the armrest of the throne as I approach.

The second born is Rargi. His hair is dark blonde, his beard brown and cut short like his brothers. We passed murals on the way to the throne room. One depicted the queen. With his lighter coloring and sculpted features, Prince Rargi looks more like the queen than any of the others.

Prince Yrgi is third born. His dark hair is worn in a knot that sits high on his head. His elbow is on the armrest of his throne, and of all the brothers he studies me the most intently, his dark eyes curious and smoldering. He is the most powerfully built, with a thick neck and thighs like tree trunks. I flush when the skirt he's wearing tents as I get closer. My sister told me this happens, that Drakoryans are lustful and the males do not hide it when the staffs between their legs grow hard with arousal. Still, it is unnerving; I wish Prince Yrgi would look away. When he doesn't, I focus on the last prince.

The youngest, Prince Oneg, looks exactly like the images of the young King Vukuris I saw on the murals. He has ebony hair, his mother's sculpted features but a stronger jaw and the same serious eyes. He wears a small goatee that frames full, sensuous lips. His eyes are dark like Prince Yrgi's, but where the third-born prince still watches intently, Prince Oneg's eyes sweep over me almost disdainfully before he looks away.

At the foot of the dais, I curtsy low and then look up at the four sons of Vukurcis.

"Do you know what it means to be a queen of the empire, child?" The oracle has moved to my side.

"No," I say, "not beyond that it is my duty to the people who saved me."

The oracle turns, speaking as much to the assembly as to me. "To be a queen is to be a mother, not just to the future king, but to the empire. The Deepening for a Drakoryan Queen is so much more than the Deepening for other brides, for she becomes the recipient of not just the knowledge of her new people, but all their cares and fears, all their hurts and hopes, all their victories and losses. The queen, above all else, understands. She is the vessel that holds, and the vessel that gives. And she will be the most loved and protected female in the Empire."

He turns to me then, earnest. "Are you ready to do your duty to the Drakoryan Empire? Are you, Zara of Branlock, ready to do your duty not just for the Drakoryans, but for your fellow humans who live under dragon rule?"

Nooooo.

I hear the word hissed in my head and with it comes a heat that makes me tense. I hear a rumble and look to the dome of the hall. Is it shaking, or is it my imagination?

"Zara of Branlock." The oracle's voice is louder. "Are you ready to do your duty, to receive the full protection of the Drakoryan Empire?"

The only word I hear is protection, and that is what I want now more than anything else as I struggle to hide the fear of the voice in my head.

"Yes," I say loudly. "Yes."

The hiss and the rumble recedes, but I still feel the emotion behind it. Somewhere, someone has heard my vow, and he is angry.

Chapter Six

PRINCE YRGI

How many maidens have my kind snatched from rocks? The time for that is over with the resettlement of our human subjects to the Drakoryan Empire. Yet in this maiden's eyes I still see the age-old fear of our kind. She knows the dual nature of the men who will claim her.

When I see how small she is, when I think of her in the dark clutches of King Seadus, of his intentions, a protective urge heats my blood. A Drakoryan's desire to protect is tied to his desire to mate. I do not know if my brothers have so intense a reaction to the small female standing before us. I only know that I cannot look away.

"Welcome to the Mountain of Kings." Bymir addresses the diminutive woman.

"Thank you, your Highness."

"Do you remember your time with the enemy, little one?"

She raises her eyes to him. "No, Your Highness. I only remember being taken."

Bymir nods. "No one will take you again. This castle is an impenetrable fortress. You will be protected here. In the Mountain of Kings, the enemy cannot reach you." He stands and everyone in the hall stand with him.

"We will fight for you now, Zara of Branlock. The victor will not only claim you, but the crown. Come nightfall, you will lie for the first time with a man. A king. Are you ready to do that duty as well? It is a vow you must make now, not just before us, but before the assembly. It is a queen's vow."

She has been instructed on what to do.

Zara of Branlock slowly turns to face the room. As she does, I can see how her long hair, the same shade as her sister's, falls in glossy red waves all the way down to her buttocks. Her posture is stiff. She knows she is to speak loudly enough so the room can hear her.

"I am prepared to do my duty as bride and as Queen for the Drakoryan Empire." There's enough force behind her words to carry them through the room, where they rebound in a small echo. Her voice seems bigger than she is, and the effort appears to have deflated her somewhat. Her shoulders slump as if in defeat. This is truly a woman ready to do her duty, but because she knows it is expected, not because she has chosen it.

"We too, are ready to do our duty." Bymir looks out at the assembly. We will take to the skies now, brother against brother. May we honor the legacy of those who battled before us."

We leave by a door behind the dais. The lords and ladies will exit through the great hall. The lords will shift into dragons in the massive tunnels and carry their ladies to the high cliffs that would take days to reach in human form. Zara of Branlock will ride with Lady Isla of Za'Vol.

For them, it will be an easy journey. For me and my brothers, it is difficult. Something changes in a Drakoryan prince when the intention to battle for bride and crown are officially announced. The lust for both physical release and power is magnified beyond what other Drakoryans feel. So is the rage.

We will each exit through different side tunnels leading to separate ledges, where we will shift just before the battle. It takes all our will not to shift in the main tunnels. As I depart, I see my brothers ahead of me in the tunnel leading to the ledges. We glance at one another with loathing. The sound of our ragged breathing echoes off the walls. Our blood is like molten fire in our veins. I can see it, glowing under my skin. I can feel the dragon pushing against this human form, eager to burst through in flame.

I grit my teeth, imagining the pleasure I would feel if they were locked on to Oneg's wing, or Bymir's throat. I clench fists that will soon be huge feet armed with curved claws, relishing the chance to slice through the vulnerable webbing of Rargi's wing. I bring my hand to my head, imagining the crown resting there. My cock bobs against my skirt. I imagine sinking it into the warmth of the trembling virgin.

Bymir has moved into the side tunnel leading to his ledge. Ahead, Oneg breaks into a sprint. I can hear him gasping. I can feel the heat off his skin from here. No words have passed between us today, but we all know our youngest brother poses the biggest threat in battle. He is eager to separate from us. He makes it his tunnel just in time. I hear him roar as he makes his way to the ledge. Rargi is the next to disappear from view. I resist the urge to pursue him into the passageway. The desire to fight is strong, and I am relieved when I find my own tunnel and see the light at the end of it.

I am almost at the ledge when the flame overtakes me. I feel it burn me from inside out, searing away my human vocal cords before I can scream from the pain. I see only the white heat and then I am the flame, sucking in the air around me as I shoot through the tunnel.

Next comes the feeling of being pulled inward, of being molded and cooled, like molten rock as they hit the water. The passageway is moist, and there's a hiss of steam as flame shapes into dragon form, solidifies. I am dragon. I am power. I am hungry for victory. I look down to see my huge clawed feet. My wings are folded tight to my body. My serpentine tail flicks behind me, striking the walls.

I emerge onto the ledge and see my brothers, their eyes reflecting the same ancient hunger. It's the hunger to rule. The hunger to mate. The hunger to win.

Chapter Seven

PRINCE ONEG

I should not have to battle them. I should not have to share their colors. They know I am the trueborn son of King Vukuris. The others may call him father, but the king sired but one, and it is me.

The cliff face curves beyond the ledge where I stand, the winter sun glinting off my scales. They are royal purple, like my brothers'. Victory will change that. When the new king is crowned, when he next shifts he will be the same gray as armor, the color of kings.

It will be me! Do you hear me? It will be me!

My mind screams to my brothers, who whip their heads around, extending their necks as they answer my challenge with roars that shake the rocks. On the viewing platform below, I catch sight of the lords and ladies. I hone my dragon sight on the tiny maiden who will be queen, but I do not care about her. A king cannot afford to be romantic, especially not in time of war. I will bed her quickly, then leave my brothers to woo and seduce the bride what I have opened with my cock. Let them ply her with patience. Let them court and flatter some silly village maiden. By then I will be in the war room, planning to avenge the death of father — *my* father!— as only a trueborn son can.

I do not wait for the others to leave their ledges. I have played this over in my mind so many times. My father once said I have a warrior's mind. He would challenge us by reciting battlefield scenarios and asking for solutions. Mine were always the best, even if he did not say so.

Today my plan is simple. Attack Yrgi, who is closest — attack him on his ledge before he takes to the air. I know what my brothers will say afterwards. They will call it unfair, but by then I will be king and I can ignore them.

Yrgi is slightly below me. I leap from my ledge, hearing the gasp of the lords and ladies as I fall at full speed towards my older brother. I extend my claws, expecting to feel them tear into the membrane of his wing.

Instead, I feel blinding pain as my feet hit rock, and a blow from above, then a second. Both Bymir and Rargi slam into me at once, knocking me from the ledge. As I fall, I see Yrgi wheel away. I barely recover before hitting a lower outcrop, and when I do, it is to the sight of my brothers, who are now battling without me, above the crowds.

Rage fills my heart, making my head pound. Theirs was a coordinated attack. They plot against me, the trueborn son of Vukurcis and rightful king! I inhale the frosty air, filling my lungs. Fire venom burns in my throat. I will set them ablaze! I will burn them to ash in the sky!

I beat my wings, pulling myself upwards through the wispy clouds that ring the peak of Mountain of Kings. I search for shapes above the clouds, and there they are. My three brothers are circling one another, angling for an opportunity to bite or claw or strike with the heavy end of a tail. They do not see me. I focus on the shape of Bymirr, eldest born and most likely the one who planned this betrayal, this....treason! I let loose with a stream of fire and am rewarded with the sound of his scream. I see him fall, trailing fire behind him as he desperately beats his wing to put out the flame.

I head straight for Rargi. He, too, must pay. I have exhaled my air and there is not enough time to refill the glands of my throat with fire venom. I will have to rely on force and rage. I make towards him, my mouth open. I aim for his upper neck, the spot right behind the head. If I bite there, I can disable his ability to make fire by crushing his venom glands. Yet before I can reach him, the air is knocked from my lungs. Something has hit me from below. Yrgi. He is repaying his brothers by attacking me. I feel myself flying backwards and scream as my back slams into the side of the mountain, dislodging a hail of rocks that slides down the side with me.

I do not immediately recover. My brothers are circling one another once more. To my fury, Bymir seems unfazed by my attack. He and Rargi are slashing at one another. Yrgi is zipping below them. I know what he's waiting for. I don't interfere. When Bymir slashes Rargi's wing with his claw, the second born brother falls. Yrgi goes for the second attack, grabbing Rargi's tail and raking his body with one bloody slash. Rargi is in a spin. He beats his wings with just enough force to find the mountainside, where he hangs on with wing and claw. Bymir wheels back, blasting fire on the rock above him, dislodging hot boulders that cascade in a landslide towards Rargi. It is too much. Rargi pulls himself to a ledge just in time to escape the boulders and shifts back into his human form.

The battle has claimed its first prince.

Now three remain. I head towards Bymir, still stung by what feels like betrayal. He is expecting this, and barrels towards me, hitting me with a full body blow that sends both of us reeling. Yrgi has swooped under us and snags Bymir as he falls. They lock talons, grappling as they spiral towards the earth.

This is my chance. I turn, diving down, inhaling air as I plummet. My wings are folded. I move faster and faster, filling my fire glands as they come into view. I will burn them. I will burn them both. I open my mouth, exhaling flame, but just as I do they break apart. The flame hits something solid below a cloud. It's an outcrop. I slam into the super-heated surface, broken and screaming in pain. When the burning doesn't stop, I realize the horrible truth. I am shifting back into my human form. I have lost.

I will not be king like my father.

Chapter Eight

ZARA

The screams of dragons. I can hear them as they battle. Heat of fire. I can feel it rising from where the last one fell. They are all the same color, except for the spines along their back.

"Prince Oneg has fallen!" someone calls when he doesn't rise from the ravine. The last two — Bymir and Yrgi— are rumbling as they rise to circle one another intently. I look to those around me. Everyone looks afraid, even the lords. But my fear is different. It's taken all the courage I can muster not to push my way through the crowd and flee back into the castle, to find a dark place to hide. Each dragon cry, each burst of heat, evokes a flash of memories I have been trying to keep at bay.

I feel a warm hand take mine. Isla puts her arm around me. "They are fierce, but they will be gentle with you. I promise."

I want so much to believe her. I wish I were so brave. Isla knows the power of the ShadowFell. She watched one destroy our village and take me and the others away. She was able to separate the dark dragons who brought pain into her life from the Drakoryan dragons who saved her and made her their mate. But seeing the ferocity of the dragons as they battle for the crown triggers whatever it is that my mind has suppressed to keep me sane. I close my eyes, and when I hear the threatening rumble of the last two dragons, I see an image of glowing red eyes staring up from the deep of a dark chasm. When I feel the heat of the battle fire, I remember what it was like to be consumed without dying.

"No," I say, and my sister hugs me once more.

"I promise," she says again.

A scream resounds through the canyon. The dragons have latched on to one another again, this time with tooth and talon. They rip and pull, throwing sprays of blood that fall just short of showering the viewing platform. In my peripheral vision, I see one of the lords of Fra'hir pivot a sickly looking Lyla away from the spectacle. The air in the ravine is rent with screams. The two brother combatants bash themselves against cliff faces, dislodging boulders and trees. They slide down the mountain amid a pile of rubble, each scrabbling for advantage. No sooner does one have it than another reclaims supremacy.

"This will end in death," one lord says.

"No it won't." At the front of the stone railing, only Ezador is calm. "It is nearly over now."

It is Yrgi who makes the mistake. He takes off, no doubt seeking to attack from the air. But as he does, Bymir's mighty jaws grab his tail, and even from here we can hear the crunch of bone as he breaks it in the middle. A dragon's tail is its rudder, and while Yrgi can fly, he cannot steer. His tail hangs like ballast. It is all he can do to stay airborne. Bymir does not attack. He knows he doesn't have to. He watches as his younger brother sinks down to settle on a lower ledge, wailing in defeat as he shifts.

The crowd erupts around me, cheering, raising their fists. Like his brothers, Bymir changes back into his human form, but unlike his brothers, he doesn't stay human. He shifts again, this time with a steel-gray flame and when he transforms into his dragon form once more, he is the color of a fresh sword blade, but with gold-tinted horns and spines.

"The king is dead! Long live the King! Long live King Bymir!" The crowd calls out to their new liege as one, and the King Bymir the Dragon answers with a jubilant roar.

Even if I could run, I wouldn't be able to. Fear has made rocks of my feet. I can only stare at the huge dragon, knowing he will make me a woman this night.

Chapter Nine

KING BYMIR

In the times past, the crowning of a new Drakoryan King would have been accompanied by days of lavish feasting.

Much has changed. While there won't be days of feasting, there will be a feast. The Mountain of Kings has its own storehouse, and there is a privilege that comes with command. Even before the battle of brothers began,, the lower part of the castle was a bustle of activity as hundreds from the serving class worked in the kitchen.

"My king." Ezador greets me with a smile when I exit the tunnel back to the main passage. "The Great Hall has been readied for the guests. Banners from all the Drakoryan houses have been hung; logs have been cut and hauled to fireplaces, and wine has been hauled up by the barrel for this one night." He stops and turns to me. "There is no need to fear the enemy will strike this night, nor any night soon. All the signs show a lull in the war, at least for now."

"As I expected," I reply. "It's one thing to steal the deep magic necessary to change dragon to man and back again; now the ShadowFell need to master the art of shifting, of controlling the transformation."

"Not an hour into your reign and you already display remarkable wisdom," the oracle says.

"Thank you, Ezador. Like my father and the other kings, you are as much a part of the kingdom's success as we are." I pause. "If only we could follow the enemy to their lair and destroy them before they return. Any progress on that front?"

He shakes his head sadly. "I fear not. Whatever magic the ShadowFell use to hide themselves is not easily penetrated. They go where we cannot follow."

We stop outside my chamber where I will dress for the feast and coronation. It's the same chamber where I will claim first rights to Zara of Branlock, who will be Queen Zara by morning. I pause, wondering if perhaps she has some clue where she was held. Perhaps she can help us find the ShadowFell.

"A word of advice, Your Highness?" Ezador pulls me from my thoughts. He arches a brow. "Focus on your little queen's pleasure tonight. Pull forth her passion, not information."

"Stop reading my mind, thief of thoughts." I grin as I scold him.

"King Bymir, that's what I do!" He taps his temple. "You'll be glad of it come morning."

He turns away without another word and I find my chamber, where a servant washes me down and helps me into a fresh skirt and a king's tunic of purple and gray, with a belt stamped with the king's insignia.

I'm not one for gazing at my own reflection. That is more Ezador's occupation. But today I do. Once I'm dressed, I look into the mirror. I am proud to be king, but more than that I am relieved. I would have been disappointed to have lost to Rargi or Yrgi, although either would have made a good king. I would have been more troubled to have lost to Oneg, who wanted the crown more than all of us combined. All four of us loved King Vukuris. All considered him our primary father, even if he was not our sire, for that is the way of royal families. But Oneg believed blood should decide the throne, not combat. He grumbled about it often enough, and when he did, our father the king would simply tell him a Drakoryan who wants something badly enough should be prepared to fight and win.

Oneg spent an inordinate amount of time studying past battles for maidens and crowns. He flew carrying boulders to build his strength. He practiced directing his fire at targets. All dragons train; it is a matter of being combat ready. But Oneg was obsessed with battling not some enemy, but his own brothers.

He and the others will soon be returning from the healing pools to prepare for the feast. Soon we will reunite in the Great Hall, and I hope that our youngest brother will have accepted his destiny.

I also hope that the woman I'm about to see understands hers.

The king can go anywhere he wants in the castle. He is the only male allowed to walk directly into the queen's quarters, although he still must ask permission to enter the Queen's inner sanctum.

I am glad that Isla of Za'Vol is here to lend support to her younger sister. From near starvation to becoming queen, the changes that have befallen Zara of Branlock's life from the time she was taken by the ShadowFell are nothing short of drastic. I'm certain all the attention must be overwhelming, too.

The walls of the Castle here are all rose quartz, with carved archways and natural pools. Veins of gold run through the floor beneath my feet. As I pass, servants drop to one knee. But outside an ornately carved door, two older women who are assigned as personal maids to the young queen step in front of me. They have been apprised of the new protocol, and I am impressed that they so eagerly take up the task.

"Good maids," I say, "I seek an audience with the young queen. Will she see her king?"

"She is dressing for the feast," says one, peering at me from under her wimple as if I am some green suitor appearing with a handful of wildflowers. But at the nudging of her companion, she turns. "I'll check," she mutters.

And so I, the king, wait for permission from a village girl to enter a room in my own castle.

Chapter Ten

ZARA

I feel like one of the dolls my mother used to make for me and Isla each year after harvest. They were fashioned from corn leaves, and Isla and I would make dresses for them out of bits of fabric.

"Hold up your arms," I would say to the doll, bending the twig limbs upward. Then I'd slip the carefully pieced-together dress over its head and tell the doll how beautiful it looked.

I'm just as stiff and silent as the ladies and maids rub my body with scented oils before fastening me into a golden dress. My hair is brushed until it glows like a summer sunset, but my face is as pale as the moon. Isla's face is just worried. She wants me to be happy. She wants me to smile. I suspect that as much as she loves me, part of her is slightly angry that I'm not happy. I have lost count of how many times she's told me how lucky I am, how any woman in the village would give their lives to be in my place.

Would they have up given their dreamless nights? Their sense of peace? I long to ask her this. I long to tell her of being captured by the ShadowFell, of horrific memories that pounce on me like dark creatures lurking in the recesses of my mind. I want to tell her that if this is the price I must pay, I'd happily trade places with any woman.

If I were stronger I would, but I have used all my strength to survive things I can't even fully remember, and now life is like a river pulling me along as I bob with my head above water.

"The king seeks an audience with you." A serious looking maid walks over to issue the news in a clipped and officious tone. "Will you see him?"

I want to ask why they are asking me, then Isla smiles and reminds me that in the queen's chambers, I am free to say no. I can't think of a reason to refuse him, though, so I say I will see him. As as the doors open, the women all but flee like deer before an approaching wolven.

King Bymir is even taller even than he appeared on the dais. He towers over me, as broad as I am dainty, as bold as I am shy.

"Zara of Branlock." His eyes sweep over me. "What a slip of a thing you are." He could be talking to himself as much as to me, so I don't respond. He reaches out, putting a finger under my chin and tipping it upwards until I'm looking up at him. "I do believe you will be the smallest queen the empire has ever seen." He smiles. "But you will grow into your role, just as I will grow into mine."

"I don't think you can grow anymore," I say, and gasp at my own boldness. The king, however, throws back his leonine head and laughs.

Then he winks at me. "Tonight after the feast, you'll come to my bedchamber and I'll prove you wrong." He steps back and bows. "I'll be waiting outside your chamber to escort you to the throne room, then to the hall for feasting." He exits without another word, leaving me standing there perplexed. The women rush back in as soon as he's gone, fussing over my dress.

"What did he say to you?" Isla is eager to know.

"He said I was small," I reply, and leave the rest of his comment out because it seemed cryptic and I don't want to listen to her fuss over what it might mean.

"Is that all?" She searches my face, as if hoping for more, but it's easy to ignore her with the other ladies flitting about like bees on a gilded flower. Everyone wants to add their own touch. A hand curls a lock of my hair; another hand smooths my hem. Fingers pinch my cheeks to bring out my color.

Then it is time and I am walked out to where the king is waiting. He holds out his arm, and for the first time, I touch the man who will be the first of four brothers to take me. King or no, the thought of it sets off fluttering in my stomach. He guides me through the castle, asking me several times if I am well. I nod, wondering whether he finds me too taciturn, but relieved that he does not push me to make small talk. I can smell the food long before we reach the hall. My stomach growls, and I am mortified when King Bymir looks down. He chuckles at my distress, however.

"I like a woman with an appetite," he says. "Tonight is a feast night, which is rare in such times. Everyone will gorge themselves. And even if you feel eyes on you, do not feel that you have to eat like a bird. I know this is fashionable for ladies, but the only opinions that matter now are those of me and my brothers, no? As beautiful as you are, the extra cushioning will serve us all well come winter. There's nothing like a plush woman to warm a cold bed."

"So you've had women, then?" I ask.

He smiles. "Yes, but from now on it is only you."

"I have never been with a man."

"That is good to hear. If you had, I'd hunt him down as a dragon and eat him."

When I gasp in horror, he laughs. "I jest. While I am glad you are a virgin, I would not kill someone who touched you in the past. But understand, if any man other than one of my brothers tries from this day forward, he will feel the dragon's fire." He nods ahead of us. "Enough of talk. We are at the hall."

The doors open to the sound of trumpet fanfare. A sea of faces stares in our direction. The urge to run away is strong, but King Bymir seems to understand and squeezes my hand. I feel I am back in my dream, but a different one. As we pass, everyone bends the knee, not just to the king but to me. My own sister and her lords, as well Lady Thera, who healed me after her lord husbands found me wandering in the forest—all bow before me.

Up on the dais are the thrones, arranged differently now. There are still five thrones. The king's throne still sits with the crown resting in the seat. But beside it is a smaller ornate throne, with a feminine version of the king's royal headpiece. Off to the side are the other three thrones, each with a defeated brother standing beside it. They are dressed in the royal purple of their dragon color.

King Bymir leads me up the short flight of steps and we stand as Ezador lifts the king's crown from the seat. I look up as he places it on Bymir's head. Ezador then takes the smaller crown. He smiles at me as he places it on my head. Physically, it is not as heavy as it looks, but I feel a different kind of weight and wonder whether I can bear it.

King Bymir pivots me to face his brothers now. Prince Rargi and Prince Yrgi are smiling, but Prince Oneg is not.

"Will you kneel before your king?" The oracle asks Bymir's brothers.

The three step forward, and I cannot help but note the effort it seems to take Prince Oneg. As the others bend the knee, he has to force himself down. He does not look at his brother. He does not look at me. He looks past us, and I glance up to see King Bymir's eyes register concern. He looks to the other brothers then, smiling, my cue that I should, too. And so I do, and they smile back, so I focus on them.

Ezador turns to the assembled lords and ladies, repeating what was said after the dragon battle. "The king is dead. Long live the king! Long live King Bymir!" What he adds feels like a dream, and makes the crown even heavier. "And long live Queen Zara! Long may she reign at his side!"

I am queen. It is not a dream. It is real.

Chapter Eleven

PRINCE YRGI

I am proud to bend the knee to Bymir. True, I wanted the kingship. We all did. But a son does not have to be trueborn to be most like the king, and our eldest brother is the most like our father king in his heart. Bymir has the quiet wit and thoughtful manner of Vukuris. True, he possesses passion and pride, but he subverts these qualities when needed. The same cannot be said for the rest of us, and now that the battle is over, I am confident that this was a choice our fallen king would approve of.

Rargi feels the same. We know Oneg does not, but pay his jealousy no heed.. In every battle of brothers—be it for first rights or a crown—there can only be one winner. Losing is a humbling experience, but one shared by the majority. It teaches humility. It restores order. The sting of defeat heals, especially in times like these when unity is important. We ignore Oneg's sour looks as we rise to embrace our brother, and also to embrace the queen. When my turn comes, I am surprised at how delicate she feels.

"Don't break her before my turn comes, King Bymir," I tease. He smiles, and she flushes deeply, reminding me she is from a more modest culture. In time, she will get used to our ways. With four mates to please, she will be naked more often than not. She will have to learn to endure salty tongues that say and do lewd things she's unaccustomed to.

The feast proves a good distraction. Once we move to the feast hall, a chorus of delighted cries fills the huge room as the lords and ladies see the laden tables. Huge platters of raised mutton surrounded by buttered carrots, turnips, and beets grace platters lining each table, sharing space with roasted boar, baked rabbit, and pork and venison pies.

Huge tureens hold varieties of soups and stews, from fish chowders to creamy soup made from pumpkin and squash flavored with cardamom and pepper sauce. There's duck and chicken and trout and quail, and dried fruit stewed and poached or blended into sweet cream puddings.

Compared to other feasts, this is meager. But for a people who have dealt with famine, war, and the death of a king, it's more than ample. For our the newly crowned Queen Zara, even the king's description does not seem to prepare her for the bounty.

"There's too much to choose from," she says. I am fortunate enough to sit to her left. The king is to her right. Rargi is on the other side of the king, and Oneg is to my other side.

"Try some of everything." I pile her plate with quail and poached pears and black bread and pork pie as Rargi adds buttered carrots and stewed rabbit. Soon she is objecting, telling us that she can't possibly hold it all.

"You'll need your strength," Rargi says, smiling. He turns to Oneg. "Tell her, brother. She has much to look forward to."

I know Rargi is hoping to draw Oneg into conversation, but our youngest brother barely acknowledges the queen we are doting on. He does nothing to put her at ease, and I can see this is already bothering Bymir.

I fix our younger brother with a firm stare. "What's done is done, Oneg," I say quietly. "You aren't the only one who lost today, but Bymir is the king. He expects you to put the queen at ease."

Oneg's initial response is silent. He takes a bite of bread and chews it sullenly while looking at Zara.

"Go on," Rargi says. "You've barely spoken to her. Make a bit of conversation, at least."

"Very well." Oneg turns and calls out. "Queen Zara!"

She turns at the sound of her name, surprised to be addressed by the youngest prince who so far has had nothing to say. She smiles shyly.

"So," Oneg says. "When the ShadowFell took you, did you know they would use you to house the magic necessary to destroy the Mystic Mountain? Do you feel any shame, knowing that trying to protect that magic drew my father to his death? And here you sit, a direct recipient of the enemy's dark deception..."

Oneg has spoken loud enough for all to hear. The entire table falls quiet, the resulting hush covering the room like a blanket. The only sounds are quiet murmurs as voices repeat the offensive words for those who did not hear them. The traveling news is accompanied by soft gasps of outrage as whispers replace the sounds of merry feasting.

Our brother king stands. He puts a hand on the shoulder of our new queen, whose face has drained of color.

"Prince Oneg." Bymir's deep voice is loud enough for all to hear both his words and the warning they convey. "We have long been without strong drink, and it seems the little you've enjoyed has already fogged your mind and loosened your tongue. Why else would you risk the ire of your king by speaking hurtful words to his queen?"

His choice of words is by design. Bymir is reminding Oneg of his authority. His eyes glow gold and the lords and ladies of the empire hold their collective breaths.

Bymir leans over, putting a hand on the table. He keeps his other hand on the queen's shoulder, his gaze fixed on our youngest brother.

"Beg her pardon, Oneg. Or by the gods who made our kind, you will beg for your life this night."

Oneg looks to me and then to Rargi, but he finds no sympathy in our eyes. We are as angry as Bymir, but for now, the king's rebuke is enough. Oneg has gotten the message; if he persists, he will face the wrath of not just our brother king, but of his other brothers as well.

"Queen Zara." He speaks her name slowly, as if it is being dragged from him by force. "The king is right. I misspoke. I beg your forgiveness."

The little queen sits silent and pale.

"He begs your forgiveness." Bymir prompts her to reply with a gentle squeeze to her shoulder.

"You have my forgiveness, Prince Oneg" she says, and although her words are spoken quietly, they ring through the hall. "How could I offer anything but mercy to someone so terribly deluded?"

The barb hits its mark, judging by his uncomfortable expression. I feel a stab of jealousy that Bymir has won her. There is more to Zara than meets the eyes. Our mate has a spine, and a quiet courage.

But this is the king's night, so I concentrate on enjoying her company now until my turn comes to get her alone. I reach out and pluck a berry tart from the tray of a serving girl, and hold it out to the queen.

"Have you tried this?" I'm eager to distract her from what has just happened.

She looks down at a plate still filled with savory food. "I have yet to finish this."

"Ah, but that's the best thing about a feast. You can eat anything you want, when you want it." I break open the tart, letting the juice run over my fingers. "These are my favorites. When I was a lad I'd sneak into the kitchen before a feast and eat a dozen. I don't know what was worse, my mother's fury or the bellyache."

She smiles shyly. "Was it worth it?"

"Absolutely."

Her thin fingers reach out and take half the tart. My eyes are riveted to her pink lips as they open. She nibbles the tart, and her large green eyes grow larger.

"Oh, it tastes of summer."

"It's the lemon," I say conspiratorially. "The cook once told me that's the secret."

"Perhaps she can teach me to make them."

"You're a queen now. You'll never have to cook again."

"I like to cook. I cooked a lot in the village." She pops a finger in her mouth to lick off some of the berry juice, and I feel my cock stir beneath my skirt. I also feel a wave of heat and look over to see Bymir staring hard at both of us. He is already feeling the possessive urge of a chosen first mate. He knows I'm just talking to Zara, but even that is difficult for him in this moment. I turn back to her.

"What did you cook?" Rargi is leaning over now, listening in on the conversation.

"Oatcakes. Rabbit stew. Baked trout when father could catch them. He was a terrible fisherman." She smiles at the memory, then a wave of pain comes over her face. "He was a good man. My mother was good, too. I miss them."

"I know. I'm sorry for what happened to your village and your people."

"Yes." She sighs. "It's just me and Isla now."

"Your Majesty." I capture her eyes with mine. "No. It's not just you and your sister. My brothers and I are your family, too, along with the sons you will give us. One day, you will be the mother of a king. Think of how your mother and father must be smiling in the Sunlit Isle."

"And yet my children will not join them." She pauses. "Isla says the Drakoryan do not go to the Sunlit Isle because of the curse." She looks sad again.

My brother the king has turned to talk to someone farther down the table, so I take the opportunity of his distraction to brush my hand over hers. "This is true. While we have exceptionally long lives, we are not promised eternity, and so Drakoryans treat every day as a treasure, as if it may be our last."

I would be happy to keep talking to her, but Rargi is rising now to make a toast to the king and queen. It is customary for the princes to toast the victorious brother king and their shared queen mate. He vows his loyalty as brother and prince to the king, and vows his protection and fealty to Zara.

I follow with a toast, vowing my protection—my life if necessary—to preserve theirs.

Cheers follow each toast. Then Oneg rises and the room falls into a hush. He lifts his cup, and vows loyalty and protection, but not to the king and queen. "I vow to always preserve the Drakoryan Empire, as did my father." He holds the glass up towards the room before draining it and sinking back into his chair.

Even if the snub is obvious, Bymir ignores it. Just as there was power in his confrontation with Oneg, there is power in his dismissal of our youngest brother's slight. As the last of the wine is brought out, he turns his attention solely to the queen, an obvious sign that the king is now focusing on the night ahead with the virgin he's claimed along with his crown.

At his side, two brothers are merely envious. But the other is seething with something more.

Chapter Twelve

QUEEN ZARA

The wine glass by my plate is still full. Isla had suggested drinking a bit at the end of the feast. It would help, she said, with my nervousness. But when the king announced that he and his queen would be retiring for the evening, I was glad I had not. My legs were suddenly shaky. Had I taken the strong drink I don't think they would have carried me back to my chamber, where I now am being prepared to rejoin the king.

The mood is different than before the coronation. Ladies select-ed to attend me remove my gown and replace it with diaphanous floor-length shift that flows loose around my body. It's as soft and white as a cloud. The scoop neck shows the tops of my small breasts. I remember how the village boys looked with longing at the girls with swaying hips and full breasts. My body is still so slim. Will the king be pleased?

"Do not worry." Isla takes my face in her hands, and I can tell she knows what I'm thinking. "You're beautiful. He couldn't take his eyes off of you. None of them could."

"Except for Oneg. When he did look at me, it was with contempt."

My sister frowns and picks up a silver brush. "He's angry at having lost, Zara. It happens in every battle of brothers, even among my lords. They will sort it out. Sit."

She guides me to a small table and settles me in front of the looking glass. As she brushes my hair, I take stock of my reflection. My pale face with its high cheekbones, my eyes so large and innocent of what is to come.

"Tell me of the act, Isla." I ask quietly, embarrassed that others might overhear. Behind me, the reflected image of my sister smiles.

"Drakoryans are different from human men." She leans down, putting her hand on my shoulders. "The fire of the dragon feeds their prowess. Each brother will put a cock between your legs that brings its own unique pleasure. A village woman marries a single man, and that is the man she gets every night. A Drakoryan bride? She marries several men, and each one is capable of doing different and wondrous things each time she's with him. Do not be afraid, little sister. Open yourself to what they offer you, but don't lose your power in the face of theirs. Your softness will unman them, both in and out of bed. It is your hidden strength. We know it. And they know we know it." She kisses me on the cheek. "You'll see."

Her words flow over me like water, but I'm still too nervous to drink them in.

And now it is time. The ladies are ready to escort me to King Bymir's bedchamber, and they do so with a giddy, festive air, some running ahead trailing bright ribbons, others giggling as they fluff my hair and tell me how lucky I am.

The tunnel we travel is wide, as is the massive door to the king's bedchamber. I'm reminded again that this was the first Drakoryan castle inhabited by men who could not completely control their urges to shift. I'm also reminded that the man waiting beyond the doors can change into a dragon whenever he wants.

A dragon. I hear a rumble in my ears and my body flushes with heat. *Don't do this.* A voice that rumbles like shifting rocks fills my head and I stop, putting my hands to my ears to shut it out.

"No!" I cry, and my sister clasps me, giving me a shake.

"Zara. Are you all right?"

The voice in my head is gone, and I decided I've imagined it. Her eyes are frightened, and I know she's not afraid for me so much as she's afraid I'll let her down. "I'm fine. Just a sudden moment of panic."

Isla hugs me. "When we next embrace, you'll know the mysteries of the flesh," she whispers. "King Bymir is a good man, and will be a great ruler. Let him teach you. Trust him."

The door opens and everyone, including my sister, falls back. I walk in alone.

A bedchamber, but also a dragon's lair. The room is cavernous. The bed is huge, with stone columns around it draped in red and gold velvet. A blaze is slowly consuming a whole tree in the massive fireplace. Braziers cast the chamber in golden light. The floor is laid with the skins of Wolven and Nightbears. The walls are hung with tapestries depicting artfully stitched dragons that are as big as I am.

"When I was a child, I'd sneak in here and stare at that tapestry." A deep voice comes from behind me. I startle and turn. The king is standing just a few paces away, and I wonder how someone so large can move so quietly.

"It is beautiful, Your Highness."

"So are you."

I look at the floor, not knowing what to say. King Bymir closes the distance between us and puts a finger under my chin, tipping it up until I'm looking at him.

"You're scared." He smiles. "I was, too, my first time."

"You?" I stare up at him in disbelief.

"Everyone is." He runs his hand over my hair. "She was a maid. I can't remember her name. Elna, maybe. Or Ella. I just remember she'd had many a man before me and I was afraid I'd make a fool of myself, or that she'd think me too big, or maybe not as big as some of the lords she'd had."

"Did you enjoy it?" I ask, not knowing what else to say.

"It was pleasant enough, and necessary."

"Necessary? Why? Why not wait, as women do?"

The smile widens. "The appetite of a Drakoryan doesn't allow that. He must find release as soon as manhood brings on the urge. Many a maid is happy to comply, but understand it is all schooling. Schooling and practice."

"For what?"

He trails a finger down my arm. "For you. While you live, I shall have no other. Neither will my brothers. Our desire is fixed on you alone. Can you not feel it?"

His touch is warm, almost hot. And the front of his leather skirt is lifting. I cannot help but notice. I want to ask him what is happening to him, but before I can, he takes me by the hand and leads me to the enormous bed, sweeping me up in his arms to put me there.

He steps back then and undoes his belt, dropping it to the floor before lifting his tunic over his head. Within moments he's standing there in just his leather skirt. His shoulders are broad, the muscles of his chest rise like smooth swells, tapering to a ridged abdomen. King Bymir is power personified, and I feel even smaller sitting on this huge bed watching this huge Drakoryan disrobe.

I'm glad he does not completely strip at first. I know what raises the front of his skirt. His cock. I am not ready to see this thing he will put between my legs. Neither am I ready for him to join me on the bed and reach for the hem of my shift. I cry out in surprise as he pulls it over my head. I reflexively start to cross my arms over my chest, but the king stops me, his large hands capturing my thin wrists and holding them fast.

"No." He shakes his head and gently pulls my arms down, his gaze fixed on my breasts. The look he gives me makes me shudder. "You must never hide yourself, my little queen. Looking on you is a long-awaited pleasure."

"I'm not too...small?"

"You are tiny, but passion increases the appetite. You'll soon recover your fullness, but know that I burn for you as you are; each time I looked at you tonight, I thought of how it would feel to suckle those sweet little breasts, how blissful it would be to lodge myself in your tight, quivering warmth."

"Your highness!" I flush at his frank talk, but something about his words—about being wanted—causes an odd stirring low in my belly that starts as a fluttering pulse then turns into a throb that centers between my legs.

He leans over, his mouth against my ear. "Drakoryans have heightened senses. I can see the flicker of passion in your eyes. I can smell the sweet dew forming between your white thighs."

Another shudder, this one stronger as his tongue snakes out to lick the shell of my ear. King Bymir lifts my hair, planting his lips to my neck then following the column of my throat to my sharp collarbone. He lays me back, tracing the curve of my collarbone to the center of my chest, then laps his tongue lower until his mouth is between breasts he covers with his hands.

His palms are so hot. I feel my nipples grow tight and achy, and when his fingers find those tender peaks to give them a gentle twist, it's as if an invisible chord reaching from my breasts to the achy place between my legs as if tugged. The throb intensifies, and I gasp.

"What is happening?" I ask. I'm suddenly afraid. My body is experiencing sensations I've never felt.

"It's passion, little queen. Your body calls to mine." He takes his hand and guides it under his skirt, wrapping my fingers around a warm, thick rod of flesh. "See how my body answers?"

I don't have to ask to know what I'm holding. King Bymir reaches back and unclasps his leather skirt. It falls, and I am able to look at what I'm grasping in my hand. It's huge, thick, and growing warmer. The surface seems to pulse like a living thing. The flared head reminds me of a battering ram. And that's what it is. He will breach me with this thing. But I cannot understand how this will happen.

"You'll tear me apart. If you put this in me, I'll surely die!"

"You will, but it will be a small death, my virgin queen, and you'll come back a woman."

"What?" I glance up at him, stricken, but he's already lowering me to the bed.

"Hush now. Let me show you."

I'm trembling like a leaf in the wind as this huge, naked king looms over me, his hot hands moving over the surface of my body. He's soothing me, gentling me and the achy little throb between my legs is beginning again and grows stronger when his hands travel to my lower belly.

"Show yourself to me." King Bymir parts my thighs. I couldn't resist him even if I wanted to, and despite my fear I don't want to resist him. He spreads my legs, revealing the mound of my virgin pussy, the outer lips pressed together, the seam of them yet unbreached. He will be my first. Bymir reaches down. I feel his finger delve into my slit, sliding over the inner folds, moving up until he touches a spot that makes me cry out and arch my back.

He smiles down at me. "The bud of your pleasure is hidden beneath a tiny hood. I will coax it out. Tell me what you feel. Your king commands it."

The authority in his voice sends a shudder through me. I close my eyes. He's shifting on the bed. I feel hot breath against the mound of my pussy. My eyes fly open. His head is between my legs. What is he doing? I close my eyes again. I want to ask, but the words die in my throat when his tongue traces the path his finger just took, sliding up through my slit.

I remember his order. "I...oh...by the gods! I feel...hot...pulsing...a heartbeat...but not in my chest...there. Down there! Oh! Stop, my king! I cannot take such a feeling!"

He does not stop. Instead, Bymir slides his huge hands underneath me to cup my buttocks. He tugs me towards his mouth. He's lapping greedily now. I feel wetness flow with my pleasure. The little bud he's so masterfully stroked with finger and tongue is now captured in a gentle sucking bite. I scream. The throb has become a quake that becomes something indescribable. A shattering. I sink and swirl into a void. I'm dying. He's killing me.

But no, I'm still here.

His body slides up over mine. His face is slick and smells of sweet musk. Bymir tells me this is my essence, and it is good. He kisses me, his tongue sweeping through my mouth. I taste myself, taste my own arousal.

"You must be brave." He is between my legs, his hand moving between us to fist his giant cock. I stare down. It's too big. But in his hand it seems to change shape, become thinner. He slides into me. It does not hurt. Then I feel it. His cock is growing, swelling, pulsing. I wriggle beneath him, but he holds me fast, whispering wait, wait...There is a moment of pain, but my cry is lost in the mouth that covers mine.

He begins to move and the discomfort recedes, replaced by a throb in my pussy that cries out for more. His movements are steady. My body, clumsy to this new bliss, tries to find the rhythm. Bymir helps me, his hands beneath me as he guides me.

I understand now. I feel something winding inside of me, a delicious tension coiling more and more with each increasingly hard thrust. I wrap my arms around his shoulders, moaning in a voice I'd never recognize as mine.

"My little queen. So sweet. So passionate." Deep whispers fill my ear, fill my heart. He's so strong, yet so gentle. He is thrusting faster. The coil of tension releases, sending rushes of pleasure through my body that are so strong everything momentarily goes black. My last memory before opening my eyes is going weak in the strong arms that hold me.

He's smiling down into my eyes. My mate. My lover. My king. I understand now. The pleasure I felt, that was the tiny death. He has spent inside of me, his hot seed mixing with my virgin blood and arousal. He has made me a woman. His woman.

Bymir rolls on his side, taking me into the circle of his arms. I feel entirely safe. He is my king and will protect me from everything, even the awful dreams of an experience I can't fully remember. He will make me forget. All will be well now.

I'm sure of it.

Chapter Thirteen

PRINCE RARGI

I've heard men speak of a woman losing her virginity. I think this is wrong. A woman doesn't lose her virginity. She emerges from it, like a butterfly emerging from the cocoon that restrained it.

When our brother king enters the hall with Zara after their mating, I instantly note the transformation. Queen Zara is still tiny, but she carries herself differently now. Her pale skin has more color; her green eyes contain a woman's knowing.

Not a scrap remained from the feast. In normal times, we would have the table spread for a breakfast feast today. We still eat well; this is the king's castle, after all. But there are no brimming bowls of fruit or whole roasted pigs on the table.

Queen Zara doesn't seem to notice. She's perfectly content with a fare of crusty white bread, fingerfish, and oat porridge topped with dried fruit and drizzled with honey,

"You look well this morning, Queen Zara. I trust you had a pleasant evening?"

She may no longer be a virgin, but she still flushes like one. I'm charmed, and over her head I catch Bymir's wink. I'm piling my bowl and plate high when Yrgi walks in. Next to the king, he's the happiest man in the castle at this moment, for tonight the queen will be his.

He walks over and boldly takes her hand. "Your Highness." He bows low. "You look radiant and happy." He nods at her plate. "Your appetite seems to have returned. Eat all you want. You'll need your strength."

She flushes again and shifts in her chair. I can't stop staring, especially when I notice how her nipples visibly harden beneath the fabric of her bodice. This little slip of a female is passionate.

"Has anyone seen Oneg?" Bymir turns his attention to us.

"Still abed," Yrgi says. "One of the maids said he took a flagon of wine to his room last night."

Our king brother frowns. "A headache won't improve his foul mood."

"No," I agree. "But perhaps it will give him something to focus on until tomorrow night." I glance over, aware that my comment has made the queen tense. As the first to fall in the battle of brothers, I will be the last to take her. Yrgi will have her tonight, then Oneg. Once I have taken her, we will achieve the Deepening—the sacred ritual in which our minds are joined as our bodies have joined.

With other houses, a woman is not considered bound until the Deepening has occurred. But royal families are different. We are able to crown and declare our mate and queen before we take her, for since the dawn of our kind every queen and her royal mates have Deepened. The union is considered fated and failproof. Still, I can tell it irks Bymir that our petulant brother got too far into his cups to pull himself from bed and join us at breakfast.

Queen Zara is eating a second small helping of porridge, and it's all I can do not to smile when I think of how daintily she ate the night before. But she needs more than food. As she puts her spoon down, she suppresses a yawn.

"Are you tired, my queen?" Yrgi asks.

"A bit." She smiles shyly. "I slept, but..."

"She was awakened," Bymir clarifies with a proud smile. "Twice."

"Your Majesty, please." Zara casts her eyes downward.

"There is no need to be modest." I lean over, catching her eye. "You will fuck all of us. We will speak of it with one another, of the things we do to you, of the things you do to us. We embrace the carnal arts. We enjoy them. And you are unrestrained in this regard as well. You will have your sisters and your ladies to attend you. Do not treat the subject of bedsport as something secretive or shameful."

"It was not the way in my village," Zara confides. "True, the village wives would whisper of what they did with their husbands, but they were not so open."

"You are no longer a village girl. You are Zara, Queen of the Drako-ryan Empire." The king covers his hand with hers. "And nothing makes us prouder than to have your ladies return home to their lords with tales of how the king and his prince brothers are keeping the Queen filled and satisfied." He pauses. "Do you think you can become accustomed to our ways?"

"I will try, Your Highness."

Bymir smiles reassuringly at her, then summons a maid. "The queen is in need of rest. Take her to her chambers. See that she is bathed and allowed to nap undisturbed. She will be engaged tonight, and a sleep would do her good."

Chapter Fourteen

QUEEN ZARA

Will I ever get used to having all my needs met?

With just a command, a maid hastens to guide me to my chamber, where I'm passed off to several ladies who have stayed behind for the honor of tending to me. My sister is not among them. Isla had wanted to remain, but I'd urged her to return home to her lords. She has given so much already, and I need to rely less on Isla and more on myself, anyway. She has sheltered me all our lives. I know when the ShadowFell took me how she blamed herself for hiding instead of trying to save me, although surely she'd have been killed or captured if she'd tried. I know my sister suffered with worry while I was gone, and was the one who insisted I be taken to the witches when I was found wasting away from the dark spell I was under.

Had I not gone to the witches, I'd not be queen now. I'd be dead, and the Mystic Mountain would still be closed to the enemy who used me to crack open the secret chambers where the deep magic they sought was housed.

I think of Prince Oneg's words. He is right. I directly benefited from the tragedy that ended the Drakoryan's historic protection of the Mystic Mountain. Were it not for me, the witches who relied on the Drakoryan protection and advised them in return would not have retreated Inward. Without me, the ShadowFell would not have gained the key to the humanity they craved. Were it not for the ShadowFell king wanting me for his queen, would the Drakoryans have chosen me?

If Isla had stayed, she would not have heard my concerns, not that I can voice them to anyone else. Despite how I came to be queen, or why, my station seems to please the people. In the wake of King Vukuris' death, the installation of a new king and a queen has restored something important to the people. I only hope I can live up to their expectations, to redeem myself for the guilt that I wear along with my crown.

A bath is prepared in my chamber. Natural depressions in the pink floor are fed by hot springs. I sink into the steaming water scented with rosewater and spice. My body is still delightfully sore from the king's attentions. There is a healing quality to this spring similar to that of the healing pools in the lower part of the castle. I exit the pool feeling languid and pain-free.

Before I was crowned, I had another fine room in the castle, but my new chambers are unlike anything I could ever imagine. The frame and canopy of my bed are of stone carved in a delicate vine pattern. Sheer curtains at each corner drape to the floor. The feather bed itself is topped by the downiest cover and softest pillow imaginable. I nestle in, clean and cocooned— a protected queen in her new, perfect world.

I am slumbering in minutes, my sleep restful until I am stirred awake by the sound of my name being called. I feel irritation as I am roused. My last memory is of a lady hustling everyone out and telling them I was not to be disturbed. I start to drowsily reply, sitting up in my bed, then decide I must have imagined what I'd heard, and start to drift back off to sleep.

"Zara."

I sit back up with a start. I was not mistaken. A voice is calling my name. A male voice.

I pull my blanket up to my chest. What man would be in my chamber? Then it occurs to me that it is probably Prince Yrgi, who is next to take me. I peer around the room, looking for him.

"Prince Yrgi, I am not to see you until tonight, and then I am to come to your chamber. Why are you here?"

"Zara..."

My name is more breathed than spoken. Hairs rise on the back of my neck. The voice is not Yrgi's. I clutch the blanket tighter, looking warily around the large room.

"Who's there?"

"Your mate." The voice is deep. The voice is familiar. "Your *true* mate."

I feel a whimper rise in my throat. I push myself against one of the posts, peering wildly around the room. I hear a deep rumble from a passageway. I open my mouth to scream but am too afraid to make a noise. I see red eyes in the dark, but it's not a dragon that steps out.

It's a man. He's tall, with long black hair. He wears black breeches, black boots, but no shirt. He is not as broad as the Drakoryans, but is still well-muscled. His face is sharp-featured and beautiful, if a man can be called beautiful. But his eyes...they burn with something ancient and dark and commanding.

"Don't you recognize me?"

I cannot answer. I am struck dumb, my body locked motionless on the bed. The dark man walks over to my bed at an almost leisurely pace.

"It's me, King Seadus. Have you forgotten? After my kind gained the Deep Magic to give us the power to change, I wanted to return to you. But there is an art to controlling the transformation from man to dragon and back again. It made me and my generals weak, and for now, I can only visit you in your dreams." He lunges for me, his hands catching me by the upper arms as he pulls me forward. In my mind I scream, for I can feel the burning of my skin where his hands make contact. His dark eyes flash red as his beautiful face becomes contorted with rage. "I was coming for you, but you married another. Wretched slattern! Faithless whore!" He squeezes me harder, jerking me to him so his face is inches from mine. "You let the Drakoryan king take your maidenhead. You let him take what was *mine*!"

I struggle to speak. It takes all my energy, and when I do, he seems surprised. "I told you when you were a dragon that I would never be yours." I stare into his eyes, not caring if he kills me. I will have him hear my truth. "Did I not tell you?"

His face softens. He smiles, but there is something wicked in his beauty, and I tremble when I feel his hot breath in my ear. "Yes. And I burned you for it. And I will burn you again, soon enough. I will burn you and those you love, starting with your king. I will burn his prince brothers. Then I will burn you, but only after the God of Dark Places has cast a new spell over you, one that slows your agony for days and days.

"I will kill all the lords, and give your beloved sister Isla to General Bralox, the dragon who stole you from Branlock. Then I will choose another queen, and the line of the ShadowFell will continue, stronger both as man and dragon than the Drakoryans ever were."

He moves his mouth to my forehead and kisses me. The kiss burns, but not as badly as his threat. Despite my attempts to be brave, I begin to scream. And scream. And scream. I don't stop until one of the ladies shakes me awake to tell me I've had a nightmare, and that I am fine in my own bed. Yet I remain distraught, and the king is summoned over my protests.

I have a new fear now. I cannot tell him of my dream. The empire is counting on me to be strong, not some weak woman so overwrought by dreams she cannot fulfill her duties.

I must be strong. I must be silent.

Chapter Fifteen

PRINCE YRGI

News spreads quickly in the castle. Queen Zara woke screaming from her nap, and would not easily be soothed. She could not remember the dream she had, and refused Bymir's offer to send Ezador the Wise to help recall and interpret it. Later, my brother king told me she seemed mortified to have caused a stir, and begged his forgiveness, as if she'd done something wrong.

I blame Oneg, who is still avoiding us. Zara has not spoken of her time with the ShadowFell, and likely has no memory. But she remembers being taken, and my brother's spiteful barb no doubt stirred recollection of that awful day.

How will I find her when she comes to me? I have had more women than I can count, and yet none have been so fixed in my mind as the one I will lie with tonight. I think of nothing else, and pace my chamber, waiting. When the soft rapping sounds from the other side of the door, I force myself to walk calmly to answer it.

Not since I was a green lad have I felt this way for a female. Our tiny queen is clad in a sky-blue gown so sheer that I can see the form of her lithe, pale body. The sight of her small, firm breasts with their pert nipples results in an instant cock stand. The triangle of red curls at the apex of her thighs is visible, too.

"My mate. My queen." I lead her into my room, and when the door is closed, I fall to one knee, bowing my head. Even kneeling, I am nearly as tall as she is standing.

"Rise, my prince and mate." Her voice is soft and sweet, and I am relieved that whatever terror invaded her sleep seems to have fled.

I stand and take her hand. "You look beautiful."

"The gown leaves little to the imagination." She looks down at herself. "I am not sure I would have chosen it, but the ladies assured me you would like it."

"I could hardly hide how much it pleases me."

Her pale face flames scarlet. She's noting how my cock is tenting the front of my skirt.

"In time, you become used to the power you have over your mates, Queen Zara."

"You may just call me Zara when we are alone, Prince Yrgi."

"And you may just call me Yrgi."

"Very well." She smiles, and it lights up her face. "Yrgi."

"Shall I carry you to the bed, Zara?"

She sighs. "I'd rather walk. Everything is done for me here. I'm bathed, dressed, fed. I might as well be a babe for how helpless I'm made to feel. I'm forgetting what it is like to be in control of anything."

I consider this. "Come with me; perhaps we can remedy that, at least for this night."

I turn and head to the bed. Zara follows me, looking around. "Your room is beautiful," she says. "The ceiling...it looks like a night sky with stars."

"It's onyx flecked with gold. When I was little, my brother Rargi and I fought for it. I won. I got the room and this scar." I show her a silvery line on my arm, and feel my blood grow warmer when she traces it with her finger.

"You didn't go to the healing pools?"

I shake my head. "No. I was proud of the scar. It reminded me of how hard I fought for what I wanted. They can be useful things, scars."

Zara suddenly looks away, focusing on a table by the window. "What is that?"

"It's an armillary sphere. Come. Have a look." I'd intended to have her in bed by now, but I have decided it can wait. I like her curiosity, how carefully she studies the object containing metal spheres within spheres.

"What does it do?"

"It represents the objects in the sky, and how they move. See?" I turn one of the spheres, and they all move. "I've always been fascinated by the night sky."

"That's why you wanted this room."

"Yes. I never get tired of looking at this ceiling. Or waking up to it. In the morning, we will wake up to it together."

"Yes." She glances down shyly.

"Come." I hold out my hand. Now we head to the bed, and Zara lets me lift her onto the mattress. She stares up at me, her fingers flitting along the neckline of her diaphanous gown.

"Do you want me to take off my garment?"

"Do you want to?" I give her a wink. "Tonight, you decide. You say you feel helpless, so tonight consider me your servant."

"Truly?" She grins.

"Truly."

Her teeth worry her lower lip. "Very well. You will disrobe."

"As you wish." I pull my nightshirt over my head and stand quietly as her gaze moves over my body. Even this—just her attention—has my cock rock-hard to the point of aching.

"After last night, I was wondering if you were all so...," says as she averts her gaze. "...big."

"Do you like being filled, Zara?"

If her soft "yes" is music to my ears, her next words are a symphony. "Would you remove my gown, Yrgi?"

I reach out and pull it over her head, marveling at the sight of this pale, sprite-like beauty sitting naked on my bed, her mantle of red hair spread around her.

"I await your further command. Tell me where to touch you, and how, and I will obey you with eagerness and joy."

Does she realize how her combination of boldness and trepidation increase her allure? Zara reclines, bending her legs at the knees. I stare as she parts them, resisting the urge to brush my finger across the springy curls covering her mound, to feel her shudder with need.

"Do all women get so wet?" she asks, bringing her hand to rest on her lower belly. "Even now, I feel wet. And warm."

I groan. "Would you like me to make you wetter? And warmer?"

She nods and I climb onto the bed. It's taking all my control not to unleash the dragon passion I feel, but there's something exciting about letting this tiny female take the lead. I've never had a woman do this; I've never thought to. I lean forward, covering her sweet mouth with mine. My tongue touches hers and I teach it to fence with mine as my fingers breach the seam of her pussy. Zara does not lie. She is wet and warm. I like that I can slip my finger into her without worrying over a virgin barrier. I like it even more that she raises her hips, inviting my touch, reveling in it. I feel the walls of her pussy clamp and flex on my finger. My cock strains towards her, eager to slide into her tight heat.

However, as I slide my finger from her quivering pussy, she sits up, eyeing my cock.

"You've touched me," she says boldly. "Now I want to touch you."

Is she trying to drive me mad? Surely she sees the effect she is having on me. A drop of clear fluid is already crowning the slit at the end of my cock. A promise is a promise, though. I nod, holding still as she reaches out.

Zara gasps and withdraws her hand as my cock bobs, and I laugh. "Don't worry. It won't bite." I quietly instruct her then how to cradle it in her palm, how to squeeze and move her hand up and down. She examines the length of me, commenting on the warmth, asking me if it's always hard, questioning whether my heavy balls are as sensitive as the cock in her hand.

I'm close to regretting giving this little minx all the control. She does not mean to torture me, but that's what it feels like, and when she begins to fondle my balls I find myself groaning at her exploration.

"My little queen." My voice is thick with passion. "I believe it is in your best interest to give me another command."

Her eyes are still innocent. Her words are not.

"I would like you inside of me now. I would like you to move hard and fast."

By the gods. I cannot push her back on the bed fast enough. I palm the base of my cock, reveling in her sweet whimper as I push myself inside her tight sheath. I'm so big. She is so small. But she is hot and wet and miraculously capable of accepting most of my shaft.

And here I take control, showing her my special abilities. I begin to move in and out while the surface of my cock pulses and vibrates inside her.

"Oh, my prince!" She wriggles beneath me, coming almost immediately. I grit my teeth to keep from coming, too, but I want to take her hard and long. Holding her hips, I rise to my knees, thrusting deep into her. When her first climax has ended, I lodge myself in Zara's pussy and hold still, allowing only the tip of my cock to vibrate against a hidden inner spot that drives women wild.

She is screaming now, thrashing her head back and forth. Her little body bucks against mine. I move my hand between the globes of her ass, sliding the tip of a finger into her bottom hole as I fuck her. Her sharp intake of breath lets me know she feels it, but if there was a protest on her tongue, it is drowned out by her cries of carnal bliss.

"Oh, Yrgi! Oh! Oh! Oh! You fill me so full of pleasure!"

The sweet words push me over the edge. I hold her to me, my seed pumping in hot spurts. Filling her is the most blissful experience of my life. One day I will put a son in her. Nothing seems sweeter than to imagine her swelling with my child. When I have released all I can into her, I roll onto my side. We are face to face as I study her. She smiles.

"Did that please you, Zara?"

"It did."

Her skin is flushed and rosy, but as I smooth her hair back, I notice something—a mark on her forehead. I push her hair aside. "Did you hurt yourself?" I'm surprised that I didn't notice it earlier. The splotch looks like a burn. I put my finger to it, and when I do, she tenses and then sits up. She puts her finger where mine just was, then fixes me with panicked eyes.

"Have you a looking glass, my prince?" The question is asked with a quaking voice.

I rise from the bed and walk to a table. There is a small one sitting there, and I bring it back, confused by her growing agitation. When I reach out to hand her the mirror, she snatches it away frantically and holds it up to stare at the spot.

"No..." She begins to shake her head. "No. No. No..."

"Zara, tis just a blemish. It's nothing to cry over." I sit down, seeking to comfort her, but she pulls away and leaves the bed, visibly shaking as she turns back to me.

"It's not just a blemish. It's a mark! His mark!" She puts her face in my hand. "I thought it was just a dream! Hidden memories! But it's real!"

An uneasy feeling comes over me. I leave the bed and go to her, putting my hands on her arms. "Zara, look at me. What's real? Tell me!"

When she looks up at me, tears are streaming down her face. "Oneg is right. I am not fit to be queen. The enemy has marked me. King Seadus has been coming to me in my dreams."

I am momentarily speechless with rage, not at her, but I know if I don't control myself she will think that's where it's directed. I will myself to remain calm. "Why didn't you say something?"

Zara is sobbing harder now. "The dreams started when I came to stay with Isla. I would wake up remembering...horrible things." A violent shudder shakes her body. "My sister said they were just dreams, that they would stop, and when I was told I'd be queen..." Her eyes search mine. "I could not let down those who had saved me. I am sorry."

I hug her to me. "You have nothing to be sorry for. But we can keep this secret no longer. We must take this to the king.

Chapter Sixteen

KING BYMIR

"What do you make of this, Ezador?"

We are in the oracle's tower room. This is the first time I have seen him look so grave. He'd quietly examined Zara's mark as she repeated what she'd told Yrgi.

"Isn't it obvious?" Oneg asks. "Even now she harbors the same dark magic that was used to break open the Mystic Mountain."

"Quiet," Rargi growls, but the queen sighs sadly and looks at our sullen brother.

"Perhaps Prince Oneg is right," she says. "If they did it once..."

"He is wrong." Ezador is now gazing into a bowl of misty water, divining. "There is no dark magic in the queen." He looks over at our mate. "But the enemy is able to reach her through dream magic. He seeks to punish her for mating with his enemy, but he also seeks to use her as a messenger. King Seadus taunts us with his ability to shift. The man she saw, the man who used dream magic to mark her, is the man he has become."

"And you expect me to bed a woman marked by the enemy?" Oneg walks over to me and points at Zara. "I am the trueborn son of Vukuris, and I will not have it."

"Then you will be the first prince banished from the Empire." The volume of my voice matches his and we are chest to chest now. Oneg's eyes flash with anger and hurt. He knows I mean what I say. "I will not suffer a selfish brother who would sacrifice our future for pride."

"So you would send away your own brother for sake of a ShadowFell puppet queen?" His eyes flash golden.

I feel the heat rising in my blood. This is the only room in the castle too small for dragons, and anger is bringing us to the edge of shifting. Even Ezador looks uneasy, but it is not he who pushes his way between us.

"Stop! Stop this!" Zara's small form wedges us apart. Despite the tension, she seems to have found her strength. She turns to our youngest brother. "I am *not* a puppet, Prince Oneg. I was a prisoner, used and threatened and made to survive the pain of dragon fire because I would not consent to become Seadus' queen." Then she turns to me. "I would do anything for those who saved me, but just as I will not be forced to accept the ShadowFell king, I will not see Prince Oneg forced to couple with a woman he finds abhorrent. And I will not see brother banish brother for my sake."

The room is silent for several long minutes.

"This will always be remembered as a tragic day." Ezador joins us now. "The queen must be taken in order of victory. If Oneg will not have Zara, and she will not allow this to be required, then Rargi will not be able to mate with her, either. And this queen, who has shown remarkable bravery and mercy to the prince who spurned her, will be the one facing banishment."

"Can they take another queen?" Zara's concern is for us, not for herself.

Ezador nods. "With royalty, it would be allowed to choose a new queen before a Deepening is achieved. The king's bloodline cannot die."

Zara puts her hand to her forehead. "It hurts," she says as if to herself, and it is clear to me that she is not talking about the mark as she turns and leaves without another word.

Chapter Seventeen

PRINCE ONEG

I brace myself for my brothers' judgement. It would be easy to take, given that it could not be harsher than what I feel for myself. As the door closes behind **Zara**, I realize that I have done more than break the heart of a woman who does not deserve it. Still, I am stung by how quickly Byrmir chose the queen over me.

"Yrgi, Rargi...out. I would have a word with Oneg." Byrmir orders. He turns to Ezador. "With Oneg's permission, you will stay. For counsel." He looks at me. I nod begrudgingly.

When our other two brothers have left, I point to one of two chairs. As Bymir sits in one, I settle uneasily into another.

"Am I really so easily forsaken?" I ask, then wave my own question away.

My brother king looks away for a moment. When he looks back, his expression portrays deep sadness. "Can a king beg forgiveness? Because I beg yours now."

"You?" I'm puzzled.

Bymir sighs. "That my words came in the harshness of anger does not excuse them. Neither does pressure I feel to set our house on the right course. Zara recognizes that, I think." He pauses. "You are my brother, Oneg, but you are more than just a prince. You are the one trueborn son of our father king. I know how much this crown I wear meant to you. I know how much...King Vukuris' approval meant to you."

"He'd be ashamed of me." I cast my gaze downward. "He'd be ashamed of my covetousness, my jealousy, my cruelty."

"No..." Bymir shakes his head. "He knows what it's like to want the crown. I think he would understand. And I think he'd know that a son of his blood would overcome such feelings. Oneg..." He leans over, his hand closing over mine. "You are my brother. I love you. Please forgive me."

I stand. "It's hard to do when I can't even forgive myself, Bymir. Those faults I have...they do not disappear overnight. I must be honest with myself. A man who harbors faults so deeply does not deserve to wear the crown. Perhaps that's why our father king never treated me like his son."

Bymir stands. "He did treat you like a son." His tone is kind but firm. "He just didn't treat you differently, which is what you really wanted."

I look away. We both know he speaks true. I looked like my father, walked like him, had the same mannerisms. I resented being without special favor I felt I was entitled to.

"The gods willing, we will all have sons by Zara." Bymir puts a hand on my shoulder. "Trust me when I say that you will be grateful when I treat your son the same was mine. Hmm?"

He is right, of course, but after what I have done... I must go to the queen. But will she even let me touch her?

"You could beg her pardon." Bymir is reading my mind.

"But will she grant it?" I ask.

"That is the question," Ezador adds. "You have wounded her. She will not allow herself to be a liability."

"And that is because I have made her believe that's what she is." I sink down onto a chair. "What have I done? I was so fixed on the crown, so obsessed with the belief that claiming it was my destiny..." I clench my fist and pound the seat beside me.

Our brother king is looking out the window of the oracle's chamber. "The ShadowFell have captured the magic that can turn them into men, but the fight for it weakened them. King Seadus cannot return—not yet. But he is strong enough to torment the queen in her dreams. Between that agony and what's been said in here, she doubts her abilities to rule more than ever.

"Out there is an empire that now hinges on whether you can convince the queen of her worth." He turns back. "As it turns out, Oneg—crown or no—you alone hold the power to save the Drakoryan Empire. Having mated with Zara, I can say with certainty that I will love no other. If this is not repaired, our bloodline will die."

I stand, heavy with the weight of what I have done, and with the responsibility to undo the damage I've caused. Had I not been so prideful, Zara would have been escorted to my chamber this night. As it is, I must beg entry into hers.

I have much time to think as I walk through the castle, and to reflect on the resentment and feelings of entitlement I have harbored since realizing that King Vukuris was my sire. Being the youngest Drakoryan brother is not easy. We are the last to learn to use weapons, the last to fly. We lose the most wrestling matches, and watch our brothers develop as men and dragons before it is our turn. The wait can be painful. All my childhood, the equalizer was the king. We all called him father, but inside I knew I alone was trueborn of his blood. Over time, I twisted that distinction into feelings of superiority and entitlement. I would look at my father's crown and imagine it on my head. I would look at the throne and imagine sitting in it. I could see myself as king. When I was denied it through rightful victory, I sought to sow hurt and revenge wherever I could.

Now I stand outside the private quarters of a woman I do not deserve, despite what blood flows in my veins. I rap quietly until the door to the antechamber opens a bit. Through the crack I see the face of a scowling maid glaring up at me.

"The queen is not taking visitors."

"I understand. But if you could tell her Prince Oneg urgently seeks an audience."

The scowl deepens. Queen Zara must have arrived back here in a state of distress for the maid to be so protective, or so defiant. "As I said, the queen is not taking visitors."

She goes to shut the door, but I put my hand up, preventing her. "I cannot force my way in, but I implore you. If you would just—"

"It's all right, Aliza. Let him in." The queen's voice is sad and weary from where it reaches me. I cannot see her. I move my hand. The door shuts, then opens again. The maid, an old woman with the face of a dried apple, continues to glare. When Zara kindly dismisses her, she shuffles off with a reluctant mumble.

When we are alone in her inner chamber, I bow before the queen. This is protocol, and I had dreaded doing it. But now I bend the knee with sincere humility, lowering my head as well.

"My queen. I have been selfish. I have been hurtful. I have been prideful. But most of all, I have been wrong. I have maligned you as a damaged vessel when you are stronger than any man I know. I have accused you of inviting destruction of the ShadowFell when you alone have resisted it. I am not worthy to ask you for forgiveness. I am not worthy to ask to lie with you. But I come now, the trueborn son of

King Vukuris, as a humble and broken prince begging you to repair not just me, but a house that will surely die without your mercy."

The feel of her warm hand on my head leaves me breathless with hope. She surprises me further by kneeling to take my hands. "Rise, Prince Oneg. Of course I forgive you."

I stand with her and although I am looking down at her, I feel her presence looming in the room. She is stronger and wiser than I realized, and I am humbled by kindness, arriving as it has on the heels of my cruelty.

"I have a question for you, though. And I want you to be honest." She eyes me directly. "Do you want me?"

I put my hand to her face. "When I fought, my thoughts were for the crown. When I lost my chance for that, I shut myself off from the greater treasure—you. With a second chance, my queen, I would show you how much I want you."

Zara smiles. "Then show me." Her smile fades then, and her hand moves to the mark on her forehead. "Unless this has ruined me for you."

"You are perfect." It is not just flattery. I mean what I say, and I feel unworthy. I feel less than a man in her presence.

Zara stands quietly as I reach for the ties on the front of her grown. It's heather green, the bodice bound with lacing that I now undo. She focuses on my fingers loosening her garment. The bodice, attacked to the skirt, falls to the floor, leaving her in just a chemise. When I reach for it, she gives me a little nod and lifts her arms.

I lift the shift over her head and step back, admiring her lithe body. My cock has risen in response to the sight of her. I want to make our first time pleasurable for her; I want to take her in a way that purges the hurt I've caused.

"If I could give you one thing, my queen, what would it be?"

She considers this. "I would like to feel that all is well, that I am safe, that we are all safe."

There is a chair nearby. I sit down and pull her into my lap, cradling her. "I would give you that if I could." I speak the words into her hair. "I would give my life to keep you safe, my queen." Her lips move to mine. The kiss is almost chaste in its sweetness. It makes me want her more, and when the next kiss deepens, I feel my cock rise and press against my leather skirt. It nudges the firm mounds of her bottom, and she shifts, the innocent movement making me groan.

"How did my brothers take you?"

"On the bed, lying between my legs." She pauses. "Are there other ways?"

I tip her off my lap and guide her to the bed. "I would ask you to trust me, even though I have not earned it."

Zara lets me help her up and position her on all fours with her pretty white ass facing towards me. Her bed is lower than mine. In fact, it's just the right height. I'm behind her now, and move my hands to her breasts, feeling the nipples harden in my hands. I play with them until she moans, then drop my lips to her shoulder. I push her hair aside and nibble across her shoulder and down her back. I crown each firm buttock with a little bite, and am rewarded with a whimper. When I slide my hand between her legs, I feel the slickness of her arousal. I part her bottom cheeks, lapping her labia until she's moaning, then moving my tongue upward to rim the tight rosebud of her anus. The queen gasps, but when I spread her outer pussy lips, I find the petals of her inner flower deep pink and engorged.

I stand and my cock quivers and splits into two appendages, one flattening and lathing the hood shielding the bud of her passion as the other slips into her heat-slick passage.

"Ohhhh!" She looks back, her eyes widening in surprise, her pussy already rippling along my length as her body surges towards its first climax. Seeing her pleasure increases mine. I am pleasuring my queen, and she is strong enough to submit to what I am doing to her, strong enough to yield to the dual sensations.

Zara pushes back against me as I thrust forward. My heavy balls slap against her labia. My hands grasp her hips so tightly I fear I may leave her marked, but she seems to revel in this.

"Yes, yes, yes, my prince." She's urging me onward, her body as forgiving as her nature. I feel redemption with each thrust into the welcoming body that grips my cock like a sheath. She's so tight, so sweet.

Zara lowers her upper body and arches her back, inviting me to sink even more deeply inside. I want to make it last but hold back, riding the waves of her climaxes again and again before taking my own release. As I spend, she rises, writhing on my pulsing cock, laying her head against my shoulder as she accepts my seed. And I understand that she had me take her in a way that restored my faith to be the man I was born to be.

"My prince," she says, and looks back at me.

"My queen." I stare down at her in wonder, not only because of the transformation she has wrought in me, but because the mark the enemy put on her is fading before my eyes.

Chapter Eighteen

QUEEN ZARA

H e has lost his grip. I could feel the invisible tightness that has held me since I awoke from the spell weakening as Prince Oneg claimed me. Evil feeds on ill intent. When Prince Oneg presented himself at my chamber door, I had a choice. I could either reject him and increase the pain that empowered King Seadus of the ShadowFell, or I could free myself through the gift of trust and redemption.

Now I turn to Prince Oneg. I take his face in my hands.

"You look so very much like the image of your father in the murals." As soon as I say the words I wonder if I should have. A shadow of sadness crosses his face, but passes. He smiles.

"I am his son," he says. "But so are the other princes. And now I shall join them in honoring the legacy of King Vukuris."

I touch my now-unblemished forehead. "And I will be your queen, and look forward to the day when the ShadowFell are vanquished forever."

"And they will be." He pauses. "When next I take you, it will be in my bedchamber. You have not seen it."

"I haven't." I smile. "Has a mate ever taken the queen in her chambers?"

Prince Oneg furrows his brow. "I'm not sure. I'll have to ask Ezador."

I laugh at this. "I would linger long with you, but I am expecting two ladies to attend me today."

"Yes." He nods. "Lady Lyla and Lady Thera."

"We do have time for a bath, however." I walk naked to the steaming spring and slip into the water. "Join me?"

I don't have to ask him twice. Prince Oneg walks in, reaching for me as steam swirls around us.

"Lady Lyla should not be traveling," I fret. "She is so heavily pregnant."

"Worry not. Her mates are coming with her. They seek counsel with King Bymir."

"You say his title more easily now." I make this observation cautiously.

"Yes, my queen. You've shown me that power does not lie in a crown, but within."

I'm touched. "I think we will be more than lovers, Prince Oneg. I think that we shall also be friends."

He holds me then, and we luxuriate in the water. I ask him about growing up in the castle. He tells me of its history, of hidden tunnels, of how the Mystic Mountain would hum with magic when the witches did their work. It will be that way again, he says with certainty, and I hope he is right.

When we finally dress and leave my inner chamber, Prince Oneg and I find that someone has not only left lunch for us in the anteroom, but discreetly selected perfect fare for a couple that has expended passionate energy. The youngest brother and I dine on rabbit and turnips stewed in ale sauce, cakes baked with unborn grains, and candied fruits. My appetite is practically fierce, and Oneg jokes that flesh will soon finish covering my hipbones.

He'd entered with apprehension, and leaves walking taller. No sooner has he gone than my maid enters. She acts as if nothing has happened, even though she finds me wearing only me chemise.

I'm looking forward to seeing Lady Lyla. She travels everywhere with Lady Thera now. The two have become friends. The newly mated Lady Thera was the first Drakoryan Bride not to be taken as a virgin. She was a village healer until recently. She saved my life, and will also be the one to deliver Lady Lyla's baby when the time comes.

"Which gown, my queen?" The maid has appeared with two others, each holding out one of the gowns Isla had made for me when I was in her care. I select one of midnight blue, with crisscrossed ribbons that mold it to my torso. It was loose on me when my sister had it made. I'm filling it out better now, and feel glad for it.

When I'm dressed, I make my way to the Great Hall to welcome Lady Lyla and Lady Thera. It is a happy reunion. Both women greet me with hugs and kisses. Lyla of Fra'hir looks radiant but weary, her belly enormous on her tiny frame.

Lady Thera fusses like a mother hen, asking about my health. She's pleased that I'm putting on weight. She delivers a gift from my sister, a silken wrap.

We spend the day in my chambers; we have become friends and I insist they let me play hostess. Although the king and his brothers have persistently told me these are lean times, I still consider the fare I'm able to offer Lady Lyla and Lady Thera to be sumptuous by village standards. The kitchen cooks have worked their magic to turn flour and dried fruit into delicious tarts with piping hot, sweet centers. Wedges of hard cheese, strips of salt venison, and brown bread are the more savory fare. There is even wine, although Lady Lyla declines strong drink.

As I chat with my ladies, I'm ever mindful that there is one more prince to take me before I am to be joined with my four mates in the Deepening.

"What is it like?" I ask Lyla and Thera, for I no longer have to ask about the carnal mysteries.

"The Deepening is beautiful." Lady Lyla is reclined on a soft lounge, her hands clasped over a huge belly that shifts shape as the baby moves inside her. "You experience your mates' memories, feel what they feel. You understand what has generated both joy and pain in their lives. You better understand their strengths."

"You also better understand their weaknesses and fears," Thera confides. "And they also get the same understanding of you. It is a journey through the mind, and we are fortunate to experience it. I daresay without it, I'd still find my five mates a mystery indeed."

"Five." Lyla laughs. "I am in awe of you, Thera. I can barely handle four. Even big with child I can barely keep their hands off me. When do you sleep?"

"Some nights not at all." Thera grins wickedly. "The twins do everything together."

"Everything?" I gasp. "Even *that*?"

"Even that," Thera says knowingly. "And as a woman who was once married to a human man, while I adored my husband and still do, lying with a Drakoryan is unlike lying with any other man. I sometimes feel women who go to their dragon-men as virgins don't fully appreciate how skillful they are."

Lyla turns on her side to face me. "Are you enjoying the pleasures of the flesh, Queen Zara? Or is that too forward a question?"

"No. It's not too forward. And yes. I enjoy it very much. I was worried that I'd be too small when I saw how...substantial my mates were. But they fit inside me nicely."

Both women break into peals of good-natured laughter. "Quite nicely, indeed." Thera reaches over and gives me a hug. "I am happy for you. You deserve good things."

We continue to talk as women do, discussing the son Lyla will soon have, our hopes that the ShadowFell's absence will be an extended one. Thera talks of spring. She says she sees signs that the hard winter will give way to early warmth. Already she has helped the villagers start seeds that will be small plants when the ground is ready.

We bathe in the pools, and the soreness from the delightful use of my last mate ebbs away, leaving me to think of Rargi, who will soon invite me to his bedchamber. The princes are taking me in haste, and I have no complaints. I am eager to be a fully-mated queen. I am hopeful for the Deepening and the understanding it will bring us.

When the maid comes to tell me Prince Rargi requests an audience, Thera rises first and helps Lyla to her feet. The Lady of Fra'hir jokes that she must waddle as she walks, and complains of pressure low in her belly. Lady Thera tells her she will check her once she's settled, and that a change of position is likely to help matters.

When I have seen them off, the maid prepares me to meet Rargi. He is second-born and the fairest of the brothers. There is a gentleness about him, but I know people are not always what they seem. I would have expected Prince Oneg to be aloof, but he was worshipful. I would have expected the king to be commanding, but he was kind. I would have expected Prince Yrgi to be masterful, but he let me take the lead. Even so, all so far have made me feel claimed, and the memories are already causing a throb between my legs. I will go to Prince Rargi slick from expectation, even though I don't know what awaits.

Chapter Nineteen

PRINCE RARGI

If a Drakoryan can't be victorious in the battle of brothers, at the very least he prays he will not be the first to fall. When I took to the skies, I was as full of hope and lust as my siblings, save Oneg. But as fate proved, hope and lust alone will not carry the day. The best of us won. Bymir will be a good king. It has been my lot to sit and wait as, one by one, my brothers took Queen Zara to their beds. Now it is my turn.

I try to stop myself from pacing the room, but the heat has been building in me since the battle. I've kept it under control, but today I fear it may consume me if I don't have her. She has been ensconced in her chambers with two ladies. I cannot fault her for taking her time. I try not to be impatient.

When the door opens, the woman who walks in is a bit different than the woman who greeted the last brother who took her. Zara is more confident. She knows a man's touch now. She knows what she likes. And there is something intoxicating about her; how else could Oneg have been so transformed? He went crawling to her bedchamber as a shamed man, and returned to us as rejuvenated and agreeable as I've seen him in years.

It seems impossible that this wisp of a woman could so easily enrapture my brothers who have had so many before her. I have had many a woman, too. I know that a Drakoryan's inner fire burns hottest for his true mate. Zara is beautiful, but she greets me calmly and coyly. Is she hiding her passion? I sense she is, that she wants me to draw it out.

My queen. I kneel before her, offering my fealty.

"Rise, my prince Rargi."

At her command I obey, towering over her. I am clad only in a leather shirt, she in an ivory night dress. She greeted at least one of my other brothers in a sheer garment, but this one is modest and hides all her charms. I'm eager to see her out of it, and honest enough to tell her so.

"Queen Zara, my father once said patience is the greatest virtue. I find it difficult to maintain mine with you so close. I do not want to frighten you, but I fear if I am to disrobe you, I'll tear the gown from your body."

Her surprising answer raises the temperature of my blood. "Over these past nights, I have learned that love does not have to be tender to be pleasant." She smiles. "Perhaps a queen would like to have the gown torn from her body."

I step to her. My breath is ragged in my throat.

"Your eyes." She looks up at me. "So golden."

I pull her to me more roughly than I'd intended. My hand finds the neckline of her garment. The fabric rips easily in my hands. Two pulls and it is open down the front. I look down at her little breasts, the tight nipples tilted upwards. I can already smell the hint of musk clinging to the damp curls of her pussy. She is aroused. She wants me to take her. The queen has had instruction at the hands of my brothers. She is a woman ready to be fucked hard, I think. She is a woman ready to feel the blending of the line between pleasure and pain.

To test this, I take hold of a nipple and pinch. There's a sharp intake of breath. The sensation has her rising up on her tiptoes, but even so she's still so very tiny next to me.

"Does my little queen seek to know what it is to be mastered?"

Her eyes hold the answer. They are glazed with passion. Her lips are parted. She wanted this when she walked in. Her pussy was wet from the thought of how her final claiming might push against the boundaries her body has been testing.

I lift her from the floor, letting her torn gown fall from her body, and take her to my bed. I sit down on the edge and throw her across my lap. She is not expecting this, and begins to struggle.

"No!" My voice rings with stern authority. She looks back, questioning, then her eyes widen as my large hand begins to roam her little bottom. I start with a rub, then begin to squeeze, each squeeze getting progressively harder. When her bottom is tender from the impressions of my fingers, I raise my hand and bring it down.

Queen Zara cries out in genuine pain, but just as quickly as the blow lands do I rub the heated patch of skin, massaging firmly but gently. I repeat the action, and from between her kicking legs I can see the effect it's having. Her inner thighs are slick, the folds of her engorged labia a shade pinker than her spanked bottom.

She's writhing on my lap now, crying out alternately in pain as I spank and then slip my finger between her thighs to stroke her throbbing clit. When I delve my finger into her slit, her hot, tight pussy clamps down so hard I feel as if the rock-hard cock jutting into her belly may erupt.

"Such a naughty little queen." She moans as I taunt her, pushing her sweet round ass up to meet the blows of my hand. "One must not tease a Drakoryan unless she wants her bottom to be made hot as dragon fire."

"Oh, my prince!" She pushes back against the two fingers I slide into her pussy, and I am mesmerized. Zara may be small, but she was made for fucking. She revels in it, and it's hard to marry the image of the shy, sad woman I first saw with this shameless, hot-blooded minx.

"Take me my prince. Please!" She's frantic with need, but I am not quite ready.

"Not yet, little queen." I take her off my lap and position her face down on the bed. "There's something I'd like to show you first."

She looks back at me almost warily as I go to my wardrobe and retrieve a small box. Once back at the bed, I position it in front of her and open it. Inside are glowing stones of all shapes and sizes. I point to one that is oblong, and about twice as thick as my finger.

"Pick it up," I say.

She smiles at me as she obeys, then looks at me in wonder. "It feels...alive. Like it's breathing and humming at the same time."

"Yes. These occur only in a narrow passageway in the Mystic Mountains. They are of all shapes and sizes, and the Sisterhood of the Wyrd, who have little cause for men, make good use of cockstones."

"Cock—" Her eyes widen as the reality of what I'm saying dawns on her. "So they use these instead..."

"To great satisfaction, apparently. It is said witches are as passionate as dragons." I take the stone from her hand and slide it through her slit. The queen gasps in pleasurable surprise. "But there are other places to put a cockstone besides a hungry pussy." With the stone lubricated, I press it against the tight crinkle of her bottom hole, my other hand stroking the tight bud of her clit as I increase the pressure. Zara wriggles, but does not move away. I move my hand to squeeze a still-pink ass cheek just as the resisting ring of muscles gives way to the rounded head of the pulsing stone. It sides into her, stopping where it widens at the base.

The queen is wriggling and moaning as I move behind her. I pull her to all fours and sink into her slowly. I close my eyes, willing my cock to mimic the stone. Pulsing and buzzing, it presses and vibrates against the clenching inner walls.

Her shrieks of pleasure fill the room. They are music to my ears. I may have been last to take her, but I am certain I've given my lusty little queen the most unique experience of all her mates, although I'm sure once this story reaches them, my brothers will no doubt try to top it.

I can no longer hold back. The quivering grip of her hot little pussy milks me of my seed. I hold her hips, gushing into her, marveling at her capacity for both pleasure and pain.

I have exhausted her, however, and she soon falls asleep in my arms. I lay her gently down, unable to sleep myself. I take a cloth and gently wash her clean. I remove the stone, which I'm sure will be used again.

Finally, I am able to relax as I crawl in bed beside her. No sooner do I get to sleep than there is a pounding at the door. It is a maid bearing urgent news.

Lyla of Fra'hir is in labor.

Chapter Twenty

QUEEN ZARA

The minutes I spend waiting for the maid to fetch me a gown stretch by like hours. I'm sick with worry as I dress, and hasten to the ladies' chamber at a run, my maids trailing behind me.

I see Lyla's concerned mates before I reach the ornately carved doorway. Lords Drorgros, Tythos, Imryth, and Zelki are pacing about the hall. King Bymir is with them. Even though the lords are worried, they still bend their knee when I approach.

"Rise," I say immediately. "What word of your mate? Why are you not in with her?"

Lord Drorgros speaks for his brothers. "The baby is early. Lady Lyla is afraid. It was Lady Thera's opinion that our distress would increase hers, but another female may be a comfort."

"Of course." I nod to them and the king and go inside.

The ladies chambers are not unlike the queen's chambers. There is a large anteroom, with lighted tunnels leading to smaller rooms. I hear Thera's comforting voice, and Lyla's groan, and follow the sounds to a chamber where the Lady Lyla of Fra'hir is laboring in one of the Mountain of King's famed pools.

"Lady Lyla!" I rush over and kneel by her side. "I fear this is my fault. The walk back from my chamber to here is long. You should have stayed with me..."

"No," Thera says. "There is no finding fault. A baby comes when it is ready. Lyla has gotten large. This will be a big son she births."

A spasm crosses Lyla's face. She is naked, and the large mound of her belly tightens like a knot.

"Is the pool helping?" Thera asks.

Lady Lyla nods. "Yes." She smiles at me. "I feel fortunate to be laboring here, in a castle with such strong pools. This one isn't even the strongest, but is as strong as the ones at home. I feel pressure, but little pain."

"Hush now." Thera eases Lyla back, then looks at me before disrobing and joining the laboring mother in the pool.

"Aaaahhhh!" Lyla's huge belly contracts again. The water around Lyla is tinged with blood, but Thera does not seem alarmed. She puts her hand between Lady Lyla's spread legs.

"The baby is coming fast," she announces with a reassuring smile. "I can feel the head." Thera looks Lyla in the eyes. "This world is drawing your baby from you. Let it. Help it, when you feel the urges."

"I feel it!" Lady Lyla leans forward, supported by the healer-turned-Drakoryan bride. I kneel by the pool, grasping her other hand. She squeezes hard, translating her effort and discomfort through her grip. I can see the small head bulging from between her legs. Her belly is so big. Her son must be large indeed. But when Thera moves to catch the emerging head, she looks surprised and concerned. The head is small, as is the body that follows. The healer pulls the infant from the water between Lyla's legs. It is perfectly formed, ruddy, and angry. A healthy but tiny baby boy. Thera puts the baby its mother's chest, and Lyla instantly cradles it just as another spasm of pain crosses her face then.

"She's not finished," Thera says, and our gaze move to Lady Lyra's belly, which is still far too large to contain an empty womb. "Lady Lyra," she says gently. "There is a second babe. You're to be the mother of two sons, not one. Think how pleased your lords will be."

She reaches back down between Lyla's legs, and if the Lady of Fra'hir has heard the healer. Her look of shock is followed by a spasm as another forceful contraction hits her. I marvel at her strength as she renews her effort to bear down once again. Another baby is coming. With one hand on her infant son and another reaching to again clutch mine, she pushes hard to bring the second child into the world. Thera catches this one, too.

"Well done!" The baby has slipped out face down, and Lady Thera is laughing with joy as she turns it over. "Your second son is..." She stops."

"What's wrong?" Lyla cranes her neck to look.

"It's not a son." The healer cradles the newborn, the cord still connecting it to its mother pulsing.

"Not a son?" Lyla's eyes meet hers. The infant has begun to wail, its tiny fists balled up beside its furious red face.

"No, Lady," I say. "It's a girl child!"

"A girl..." Lyla stares at the baby in disbelief, then holds out her arm. "Give her to me!" Thera lays this child on Lyla's chest beside the first infant. Her chest and upper body are above the water, and the babies are instinctively rooting around for their mother's nipples. Each finds one, which pleases Thera. The healer says the nursing will help Lyla deliver the afterbirth.

When that is done, maids who have been standing by come to assist in getting the babies cleaned up and swaddled while others are called to help the new mother be cleaned as well. All are transported by an enclosed litter back to Lady Lyra's chamber. When Lyla is tucked into bed with an infant under each arm, her lords are called in.

The looks on their faces register relief, surprise, and shock in learning they not only have two children, but that one is a daughter. I know daughters are rare in the Drakoryan Empire. They are considered natural witches, and at age three or four, have traditionally been sent to be raised by the Wyrd in the Mystic Mountain. Perhaps this is why Lady Lyla has begun to weep softly. Thera and I stand by as we listen to her tell her mates to promise not to send her daughter away.

"I was separated from my own mother once," she says. "I would never do such a thing to my own child. Promise me that we will raise her just as we raise her brother!"

Her lords gather around her, kissing her, kissing the babies.

"You do not have to worry, love," Lord Imryth says. "The witches have gone Inward. Much has changed, especially for women of the empire."

"But when they return...they will want to take her! Promise me!" Despite what she has been through, Lady Lyla is fierce in her determination to extract this vow. The Lords of Fra'hir look at one another, nodding.

"We promise to do all we can," Lord Drorgros says. "We will do what we can to keep both babies with their mother, and their fathers."

There is no discussion as to which lord fathered these children which bear the most resemblance to Tythos, who studies them intently, his eyes tearing up as he strokes their ruddy cheeks and examines their tiny hands. But even if one is the sire, all Drakoryan males treat the children in their household as their own, and the Lords of Fra'hir all gaze at the twins and their mother with the same love and affection.

"Come, let us leave them together," I say to Lady Thera, who smiles as we exit.

"Yes," she says. "They need to rest. And I believe you have something to do."

I'd almost forgotten. The Deepening. Thera knows this marked the night I was taken by the last prince. Now is the time for the final step. I look back at the babies, and consider them a sign of new beginnings for us all.

Chapter Twenty-One

QUEEN ZARA

"A daughter?"

When I come to King Bymir with the news, he's momentarily stunned into silence. The last daughter born in the kingdom was to Lady Syrene. Her little one was sent to live with the witches, and has now gone Inward with the Wyrd.

"Her lords promise to keep them together," I say. "It seems cruel that the practice has been to send the girls away."

"It is only because female Drakoryans have the gift of sight. They are natural witches, Zara. It is our way."

"I believe Lady Lyla will change your ways."

"Much has changed already." The king sighs and comes to sit beside me. After the birth, I sought him out. As queen, it was my place to deliver news of what had just happened under our own roof. I don't realize until now how confidently I am slipping into my role of power and authority. I, a former ShadowFell captive, tortured by the enemy.

I, a woman used as a pawn by the dark forces. I'm a queen now, and for the first time can see a way for myself, one that includes using my own power to defeat those who have wrought such destruction.

"How long will the witches stay Inward?" I ask.

The king shakes his head. "I know not. Neither does Ezador, although the portents seem to show it is a span of time. War may return to this land before the witches do." He pauses. "It's likely that this daughter of Fra'hir will grow up before the Wyrd come back to the Mystic Mountain." He turns to me. "That doesn't mean there's no magic in the land. Since strife has returned, we Drakoryans have seen it worked time and time again in our own households through the strength and resolve of the brides. I expect no different from you." He puts my hand to his lap. "See how you've already summoned my lust?"

His bearded face beams with a mischievous smile, which I answer by sliding my hand beneath his leather skirt. "It is not every village girl that grows up to hold the royal staff, my king."

"Indeed." He lifts me, throwing my long skirts aside as he impales me on his cock. "It is not every skinny lord who grows up to fuck a beautiful, flame-haired queen."

I'm getting better at this. I begin to move, sinking up and down on his hardness. I trace his handsome face with my fingers. The king turns his head to capture my thumb in his mouth. He nibbles and sucks on it, the sensation sending the first waves of climactic pleasure washing over me.

"My queen is easily pleased," he says.

"And my king is easily spent." I rise up suddenly and then sink down on his shaft, gripping him tightly with the walls of my pussy. King Bymir's expression registers surprise as he loses control, and I plant my laughing mouth to his as his seed floods into me in hot spurts.

He moans throughout our kiss, his hands moving up and down my body. When our lips part, he stares down at me.

"I could have you beaten for your impudence."

"I would bend over and bare my ass for it, but only if you fucked me afterwards."

He throws back his head and laughs until tears of mirth are flowing from his eyes. "Oh," he says. "What have you done with that shy, frightened virgin I brought to my bed?"

"She's changed, your majesty. She's a woman now, whose every thought is for her king, her princes, her kingdom."

"Yes," he says. "And it is time for the final step."

Chapter Twenty-Two

KING BYMIR

The Deepening is a vital part of the Drakoryan bond. It can be a hard-fought goal, and for our family, it has been no different. Jealousy, past hurts, and old rivalries are often obstacles to the full mating that must precede the final step of blending thoughts, feelings, and memories in an ancient ceremony that also allows bonded mates to communicate through thought.

As important as the Deepening is for all Drakoryan households, it is the most important for a queen and her mates.

"The Empire is only as strong as the bond of the family that rules." Those were the oft-spoken words of our fallen father and king, who now leaves us to carry on his legacy of steady rule.

We gather in Ezador's chamber for the Deepening, and I believe he is as pleased as we are. Zara, who has become so much more confident, teases the oracle that his robe is finer than her gown, and Ezador does seem to have taken the occasion to array himself with even more elegance than usual. His cobalt blue robe is embroidered with constellations sewn with enchanted threads. The star charts shift and move on the cloth, and under the robe's hood, his beautiful face shines with a celestial glow.

The queen is wearing a violet gown trimmed with silver, the neckline dipping to reveal the swell of breasts that are fuller now. Her red hair is plaited to hang down her back. Some of the hair has been threaded through with tiny gemstones so that the braid shimmers when it catches the light.

"Are you certain she is not a fey creature?" Ezador asks with a quirk of his brow, for surely no mortal can have such beauty without the aid of some sorcery. His tone is teasing, but his words are true. I can feel our shared pride as we gaze at our beautiful queen.

Ezador takes her hand and gently leads her to a chair in the center of the room, the backrest carved with a dragon scene. The arm rests are dragons, too.

"Only Drakoryan queens have settled in this chair," the oracle explain as he guides her to sitting on the cushioned seat. "Like the mountain castles, it was wrought from magic, a gift to the very first queen to celebrate a Deepening with her shared mates." When she is seated, Ezador smiles down at her. "I have known most of them, you know. They were all strong in their own way, and I mourned their passing. They are on the Sunlit Isle now, sad to be separated from their lord husbands and sons, but happy to see a new queen become the loving mother and sister to this Empire."

I see sadness pass over Zara's face, and I know it pains her to think of death separating us without hope of the reunion promised to mortals. But the hurt passes to be replaced by resolve. "I long to make them proud," she says.

"You will." Ezador nods to me and my brothers, and we approach to place our hands on Zara. He is holding the ancient book with the spell that will begin the Deepening. His voice takes on a deep timbre as he reads the words in age-old dragon tongue.

I am the first to share my life with Zara. I feel myself swirling back in time, back and back until I gasp from the pressure of being squeezed out of my mother's body. My lungs fill with air and I scream. I feel cold and hunger and somewhere in the recesses of my consciousness, I know that Zara experiences this, too. Through my eyes, she watches me grow up. She sees my small hands grapple for salamanders in the caves beneath the castle. She hears my father scold me as a nurse bandages the arm I've injured when I pretended to be a dragon and jump from a high rock. I was eight then, and father king would not let me mend it in the healing pools. He said feeling the pain would make me less likely to repeat my folly. I let her feel the agony all Drakoryans must endure, and the solitude, of the first shift. My brothers and I were so wild we had to be chained to the walls of a cavern beneath the castle, where we screamed and raged in madness. I let her feel the pain of the first shift followed by the freedom of being reborn through fire as a dragon. I let her feel the joy of flight. Through me, Zara relives the pleasures and tragedies of my life, from my first time with a woman, to the last embrace of my dying mother, to the pride in my fathers' eyes as I proved myself as a man, to the unfathomable grief and rage when I watch him die.

And I let her feel the love I have for her, a feeling that dwarfs all the other emotions. I let her feel how she has healed me, and I know she will feel it from my brothers as well.

Chapter Twenty-Three

QUEEN ZARA

It is unlike anything I could have imagined. It is a journey through the lives of the men I love. But I am not a spectator. I am the men I love, slipping through their experiences like a fish slips through a stream.

I see their characters develop from childhood. Rargi is patient from the start and slow to anger. His mother calls him her Little Rock. I toddle on his wobbly legs as he takes his first steps. He speaks full sentences and learns to read earlier than his siblings. His father, a cheerful, handsome lord, ferries him through the castle astride his broad shoulders.

"Faster, faster!" he cries, holding only the collar. Later I am him on horseback, galloping through across the Drakoryan plains. I am Rargi in his late teen years, and when the disobedient horse throws me, I shift into a dragon as I land, take flight, and pick the horse back up. The terrified animal is deposited in the stable yard and afterwards never gives me any more trouble.

As Prince Rargi, I am the first to comfort Yrgi at the death of his natural father, and openly weep at the death of my own, the last prince to die. I feel King Vukuris' hand on my shoulder, hear his voice telling me his brothers died proud because of their sons.

I feel dragon grief as — along with my brothers— I exhale fire that consumes the body of the king himself. The sense of loss is like a cold knife to my heart. I feel the fear Rargi cannot show, his fear for the future. I feel his arms around a woman—me. I feel my body against him, and feel the fear replaced by comfort and a new security. He is showing me my power to heal.

As Prince Yrgi, I feel invincible, strong. I am the fastest, the one with the most prowess. Women flock to me, and while his exploits are something most mates would not care to know about, let alone live, I understand that this is what makes him who he is. Yrgi is insatiable, visceral. I realize his letting me take the lead on our first night together was out of his character; it was a gift.

I feel his passion in other things. Through his dragon eyes I relive the battle with his brother for the onyx room, the fight that gave him the scar he still bears. In dragon form he flies for miles just to find a certain ledge where he can watch the moon rise over some distant mountain. I watch him draw star charts in his room, see him wing to distant and secret places to bring reform as a man and pluck flowers for some maiden he fancies, or for his mother.

I feel his outrage as the Mystic Mountain splits open from the inside. This is mixed with my own pain and a sudden burning aware-ness—the slip of a memory that's not his, but mine. Then the per-spective is all his again. I see King Vukuris' body tumble into the ravine through Yrgi's eyes. I hear and feel his scream in my throat.

And finally, I am Oneg, being told that there will be a queen. I feel anger at the news, and feel myself brooding in the empty throne room where I stare at the crown that used to sit on my father's head. I am trueborn. There should be no battle. The crown should be mine, and I should choose my own maiden. I am angry to have conceded to the pressure to take a woman I consider tainted by her time with the ShadowFell.

I feel Oneg's distrust for me, his disdain. I also feel the source of all his hurt and insecurities. I am him as a small boy. My mother has told me I am Vukuris' trueborn son because I have asked, as boys eventually do. I am running through the castle, feeling proud. I round a corner to see King Vukuris with is arm around Bymir, praising his swordsmanship. "I could not be more proud of a son," he is saying.

Rage forms like a ball in my stomach. I run the other way, and day by day, the ball grows. Every compliment the king pays my brothers feels like one stolen from me. I ask my father about the value of blood one day. He looks me up and down. He knows I am his trueborn, but he tells me that with Drakoryans, it is bond, not blood, that makes a Drakoryan son. He says my brothers and I are all equal to him.

He has denied the distinction, but I do not. I vow to be the biggest and strongest dragon. I vow to set myself apart. There are flashes of the king's pride, his notice of me, each accompanied by a swell of happiness followed by a letdown when I realize with each attempt that the garnered pride is no greater than what is shown to my brothers.

Through Oneg's eyes, I watch the old king die. I feel a sense of loss so great as to be crippling. But it's not the loss of a father that pains me so much as the loss of the opportunity to garner the trueborn distinction I have spent my life chasing.

Oneg lays bare his hurt; when I experience the burning of his father as a dragon, I feel myself direct fire at the body in a joint show of grief and rage. The chance to set myself apart has died along with the king.

I view myself through his eyes on the day we met. He sees me as small and waiflike and inferior. He does not trust me. He believes me unworthy of a trueborn son of Vukuris, having decided that even if the king did not recognize his greatness, he will hold fast to the pride that hardens his heart against me.

I hear the hurtful words come out of my mouth—his mouth—at the feast. I feel the weight of his brothers' anger, his alienation. The Deepening is like a confession; Oneg shares his thoughts with me knowing his brother sees them, too. The thoughts are dark. He imagines himself becoming dragon to slay them in their beds, to slay me, before taking the castle by force. When he cannot bring himself to do it, he believes this is because of the weakness his father saw in him.

Then, through him, I feel my love. It is like a balm washing over him. I listen to his heart as he realizes that true strength lies in unity, and true happiness in love. We have both been captive to monsters, only his was inside him. The night we were together, we freed one another. I feel tears of emotion course down my face at his honesty.

"We love you, brother," I hear the others tell him. Oneg is weeping. His hands on my shoulders shake.

Then come the memories of the Drakoryan Empire. My mind is bombarded with knowledge. Flashes of script appear before my mind's eye, and I can read the ancient dragon language. I hear it and understand. I see the first dragons made in the cave by the Lord and Lady. I watch their trials in this very castle. I see virgins taken from rocks to become loving ladies to Drakoryan lords. I see the subjugation of humans, both within and from beyond the mountains. I see war and fire.

It happens in an instant, this journey through time. My mind swells with the knowledge of the ages, the knowledge of what is now my people. I will tell the stories I now know by heart to my sons.

Then comes my turn to share. What do royals know of village childhood? I show them a stone cottage, and how it feels to dig one's feet into the cool dirt floor on a hot day. I show them the ache of hunger pangs when food is scarce, and the simple bliss of giggling under the blanket with my sister on a cold winter night as, across the room, our parents scolded us to hush and sleep.

I show them work. Through me, they feel the udder of a goat as milk squirts into a wooden pail. They feel the small cuts that develop on finger pads as I pick grains from heads of fall wheat. The see the longing looks of village boys as my sisters and I pass. They listen as our mother tells us not to fall in love, as we are forbidden until we are too old for the dragons to select us as mates.

I show them the fear every Drakoryan maiden feels that she will be the one led to her village's Altar Rock. As I move through my life, letting them experience it through my senses, I edge ever closer to the memories I have suppressed. I want to stop, but something is pressing me onward.

Show them.

I draw a ragged breath and let the memories come. It is a cold night. I feel my sister Isla leave the bed. My last memory is of her telling me she is going to make water. I nestle into the warm spot she left and am just drifting back off when I hear the sound of rushing wind. There are screams. Am I dreaming? No. My parents are shaking me awake. I hear the sound of timbers cracking and breaking, of stones flying and hitting our cottage. Something is happening. Something terrible.

It sounds like the end of the world.

It looks like the end of the world.

Smoke stings my eyes, causing me to gasp as we flee from our crumbling cottage. Through the choking haze, I see a huge shape. It lashes with its long tail and a burning cottage flies apart. I stare helplessly as the monstrous creature grabs a person from the ruins and slings them apart. I look down and scream. Blood stains my gown, my face, my hair.

"Isla!!!" I call for my beloved sister, then turn to my mother. But as I do, the ground shakes.

"It's a dragon!" My father calls. Those are his last words. The beast shoots another stream of flame, igniting what was our cottage. He is lost in the smoke. I hear my mother's screams join the others as she tells me to run.

I do, but I don't get far. Something is tight around my waist. I am sure I am going to die. I look down. A hand, but not human. I am in a dragon's clasp. It takes me through the haze to the edge of the village where an iron cage is filled with other dazed or screaming village girls. I am shoved inside. My head strikes one of the bars and everything grows dark. I sit up, forcing myself to recover. I look for my sister. She is not here.

I am helplessly trapped as I scream with the others. Branlock is being destroyed by a huge black dragon. It is merciless, slaughtering men, women, and children. Every cottage is reduced to smoldering rubble.

Does it take hours or minutes? Time seems irrelevant. My throat burns from smoke. I am hoarse from yelling for Isla. She could not possibly have survived. I sink to the bottom of the cage, moaning as the cage goes airborne.

All fades from black to red. I open my eyes. I am in a narrow cave. There is a ledge, but it is far above, backlit by a reddish haze. There are cracks in the walls. Through them I hear the sound of weeping women. I am in the lair of the black dragon, as are the others. We are being kept separate. From time to time, food is dropped to me. Dry bread. Salt fish. My grief is strong, but the hope that I may see Isla again is stronger. I eat. I drink water trickling from a rock.

How long am I here? I cannot tell day from night. I cannot escape. The wall beneath the ledge is too sheer, and even if I could climb it, the dragon lurks above. I can hear it breathing. I can feel the vibration of its heavy steps, hear the swish of its tail.

I sleep, and awake to hear pleadings and a low growl. I put my eye to the crack in the wall, keeping my hand over my mouth so I do not scream. I see a hooded figure. I see the dragon. I turn and sink to the ground. I sob into my arms, shaking.

Then it comes for me. At first I just see the head snaking over the ledge. Then the body follows, scaling the wall downward. It is not the same dragon as from the village. This one is larger. Its eyes glow red, the vertical pupil expanding and contracting as it stares at me. A dark wisp of smoke appears beside the dragon. A man steps out. He is wearing a black cloak. His face is ugly and twisted.

He looks at me. "Kneel," he says, "for you are in the presence of the God of Deep Places."

I do not kneel. "You are no god of mine. I will not bend the knee before anyone who stands with what destroyed my village." The hooded figure smiles. It is a cold smile, and at that same moment I feel a stabbing pain, like a knife in my belly. I collapse to the floor, screaming and writhing from agony so intense that when it subsides, I am left drained.

The hooded figure moves his hand over me. "She is the one." He looks to the dragon. "Inhale her essence. You can smell it. She has the inner magic we seek."

The dragon rumbles low in his throat. He breathes in. I feel my tattered gown and hair pulled towards him. I cry out. He shows his teeth in a horrifying smile as he tilts his head towards the hooded figure, who addresses me once more.

"This is King Seadus, the dragon soon to be made human. With your help, he will access the deep magic of the Mystic Mountain. Only one who possesses magic can be a vessel for it. Once you have aided us, King Seadus will take you as his bride."

"No." I am shaking my head.

"You must. You must consent."

"Never."

"Say you will." The menacing whisper of the God of Deep Places' mixes with the dragon king's rumble of a growl.

"No."

"Then you will be punished."

I show them the worst of it. I show them the spell that allows me to burn without dying, again and again. I pray for death that does not come, but I do not give in. I will never be his.

I am lying on a slab. I am dressed. I am in a white gown. The hooded figure stands over me. He tells the dragon he is preparing me to wander and waste away in the ancient wood. Hunger will draw the humans in to hunt. I will be found.

Through the eyes of twisted ShadowFell soldiers sent to attack the village, the evil god saw a lady there— a Drakoryan Bride. He knew then that a maiden of Branlock had survived. He knew she was of my blood. He will bring me close to death so that the only way to save me is witch magic. When I am inside the mountain, he will use the magic he puts inside me to open it to him and the ShadowFell.

He forces the magic into me. It is a different kind of pain, the kind that goes into my very soul. I scream and scream. It is worse than fire, this twisted, dark ugliness lodged inside my breast. I beg him to take it from me. I am ignored.

I am in the forest. I am cold. I am hungry. Just as fire could not consume me, neither can cold and hunger. I see water but cannot drink. I see berries but cannot raise a hand to put them to my mouth. My arms grow thin as twigs. My stomach hollows and my ribs jut from my body. I pray for a death that will not come.

I hear cries. Someone speaks of a fey creature. They are afraid. Then a big man approaches, and another. They are warm, but the warmth cannot touch me. They ask me questions, and I open my mouth to tell them my name, to ask them for help, but I only respond with mad gibberish.

I am in a hut. Warm broth runs into my mouth and out again. I cannot eat. I cannot drink. I am wasting away. And then there she is. My sister. My lovely sister. My Isla. She touches my face, kisses me, sobs. She begs me to eat. I cannot.

Dragon wings. Flying. A pool. My sister weeps. Healing waters, they say, but I float helplessly like a dried leaf. The witches. Isla begs. Someone must take me. I want to say no. I want to tell them that I house something within me, something awful, that will bring about ruin if I am taken there. I try to push the voice out of my body, but it is trapped behind the writhing black mass deep in my chest.

We are flying again. *No. No. No. No. No.*

Women. Blacked-robed. Wise. But not wise enough to see what is inside of me. They take pity. They take me in. They lower me to a pool.

I feel strength. I feel heat. I feel….life. I find my voice. I open my mouth to warn them, and my body begins to jerk as something black and hazy flies from between my lips. Screams. A flash, the sound of running. There is a popping sound, then a crack. Hands grasp me. I am pulled through a doorway that wasn't there.

I awaken in a quiet wood. There are birds. Light filters through the trees. It would be blissful but for the sadness I feel all around me. The witches are sitting in a circle. I can feel the weight of their worry. One comes to me. She is silver-haired and beautiful. I begin to apologize. I am sobbing as I explain how I tried to tell her. She puts a finger to my lips. She tells me she is Arvika, and that I am not to be troubled. She says all that happens happens for a reason. She smiles.

"The ShadowFell King does not know what he has done," she says. "He is being used as surely as you have been used. The one who aids him is no friend. She tells me war will consume the land for years, bringing great suffering and tragedy. She tells me to be strong, for my people."

"My people are dead," I say, thinking of Branlock.

"No. The Drakoryan people. You will be their queen. You must go back."

I do not want to go back. I beg her to let me stay, but she tells me the Wheel of Fate cannot be stopped. There are scores that must be settled, prophecies that must be fulfilled. My parents birthed a warrior and a queen, she says. Both Isla and I will find our destinies.

Then she leans over, and all goes black. I feel the connection with King Bymir and his brother has ended. I am alone with Queen Arvika.

A new memory comes, one that his hidden from me until this moment.

"Lady Lyla of Fra'hir is part of the prophecy, too," Arvika says. "It was foretold, and now I would have you carry a message to her. Tell her the girl child she birthed tonight will bring peace to the Drakoryan Empire. Tell her to fear not. She will raise her daughter. Tell her to look and listen for signs from the Wyrd. We cannot return, but we will speak through dreams. Tell her the girl child has a name. Her name is Sabine."

I am pulled back and back until I am sitting in my own body, in the present, with my mates. With the exception of the message meant for Lyla, they now know my story—a story that until the Deepening was even lost to me. They kneel and embrace me where I sit in my chair. They kiss my tear-stained face, and I return their kisses one by one.

Off to the side, Ezador watches, and I know that even though he was not part of the Deepening, he gleaned what transpired.

The witches did not say what the cost of the war would be. She did not say who will be lost in this war. I think of all those I now love. I have felt loss, and do not want to feel it again.

"You are queen fully now," the oracle says.

I stand, circled by my mates.

"I am ready," I say. "I am Zara, Queen of the Drakoryan Empire."

Other Books in the Drakoryan Bride Series

About The Author

USA Today bestselling author Ava Sinclair has been writing erotic romance since the late 1990's, capitalizing on the spicy readers' desire for kink long before Fifty Shades of Grey brought it mainstream.

She's written over fifty books and is enjoys weaving conflict and relatable situations into her books.

She lives on a farm in the foothill country of Virginia. When she's not writing, she's fussing over her cats or tending to her dairy goats and Shetland sheep.

Connect with Ava

L et's be friends. Hey, it's possible today thanks to social media. Here's where you can find me.

On Facebook I have a main page, an author's page – both under the name Ava Sinclair - and a private group – Ava's Risque Reading Room.

I'm also on Instagram and TikTok as **@authoringava**

Want to write me? I love hearing from readers. Reach me at eroti cabyava@gmail.com

Milton Keynes UK
Ingram Content Group UK Ltd.
UKHW020646010823
426141UK00016B/692